Death
in
the
Ring

George Thomas Clark

Published by GeorgeThomasClark.com

ISBN: 978-0-9967492-4-4 – Trade Paperback (Revised)

Copyright 2017 by George Thomas Clark

GeorgeThomasClark.com
Bakersfield, California
webmaster@GeorgeThomasClark.com

Books by George Thomas Clark

Hitler Here
The Bold Investor
Death in the Ring
Echoes from Saddam Hussein
Obama on Edge
Tales of Romance
In Other Hands
Paint it Blue
King Donald

Introduction

Let's invite many of the greatest boxers, and their contemporaries, to tell their own stories, some true, others tales based on history. Peter Jackson barges into John L. Sullivan's hotel room to demand a fight. Jim Jeffries regales listeners about his barroom confrontation with Jack Johnson. A bar owner discusses the violent alcoholism of Battling Siki. Jack Dempsey and his detractors hold forth. Sonny Liston stars in three stories. Nelson Mandela boxes Barack Obama. The top 13 heavyweights are identified. Muhammad Ali, Jerry Quarry, Emanuel Steward, Alexis Arguello, Lennox Lewis, and Archie Moore and others also share experiences. They're frank about their serious business. They know there can always be *Death in the Ring*.

Contents

Fantasies

Drinks on the Champ

A long time ago, in the early 1880s when John L. Sullivan had just become heavyweight champion, he toured the country and offered a hundred dollars or more to anyone who could last four rounds, and I decided to try him. I'd done some boxing with the neighborhood guys and was taller and heavier than Sullivan though not as muscular. After a handler laced on my gloves, I walked to the center of the ring, which was really a mat surrounded by people, and looked at the biggest, meanest face you've ever seen. Even his handlebar mustache seemed tough as steel. I decided to begin cautiously, since my goal was to survive rather than actually beat Sullivan, and jabbed at his nose. I believe I touched it, and was most encouraged, and continued jabbing until I felt an explosion. Sometime later I came to on the mat.

A couple of minutes after that I was able to stand, and Sullivan strode over and said, "No one can take my right, but I admire those who try. Come on, let's have a few."

"Thank you, sir," I said, and unsteadily joined him in a carriage with a couple of men from his group. Sullivan led us into a large saloon, bellowing hellos and shaking hands and patting shoulders, and slammed money onto the bar and roared: "I can lick any man in the room, but don't worry about that. Drinks are on me." He drank faster than anyone I've seen, and everyone gathered around to listen to the most dynamic man in the world. He grew louder each drink and beckoned some of the ladies employed by the saloon. They may not have been nice by society's standard but sure were pretty, and all of them smiled at Sullivan, who nuzzled them and winked at me and said, "Can't decide which two I want."

I think alcohol interested him more than women but quite late he did choose two and disappeared. Shortly thereafter I suffered my second knockout of the night, this one a left hook by whiskey.

Peter Jackson for Mr. Sullivan

I don't have to publicly say the somewhat older and smaller John L. Sullivan is afraid of me. A few prominent pugilists as well as candid journalists are kindly proffering that information. However much the bibulous champion may despise people of my race, he knows my strength, quickness, and grace would make me a most formidable opponent and, I should think, our meeting an inevitable consequence of public desire. I've outboxed and battered the best competitors in Australia and San Francisco, and Mr. Sullivan is the only logical man to fight after he beats Jake Kilrain during seventy-five bare knuckle rounds somewhere in rural Louisiana. My manager Charles Davies and I learn the champion is convalescing in Chicago, where I'm visiting Mr. Davies, and we hasten to the hotel.

To the innkeeper, Mr. Davies says, "Will you please tell John L. Sullivan that Peter Jackson and Charles Davies are here to see him?"

"Just a moment."

He walks up the stairs and soon returns to say, "Mr. Sullivan is busy and will not be receiving you."

"Do you suppose that Mr. Sullivan will ever receive Mr. Jackson?" asks Mr. Davies.

The innkeeper misses the irony, I think, and returns to his life behind the counter.

As if divinely prompted, Mr. Davies and I nod at each other and march up the stairs.

"Gentlemen, wait…"

We ignore him and walk straight to a door where a large pudgy man stands.

"Peter Jackson to see Mr. Sullivan," I say.

"He already said he doesn't want to."

"Sir, I've come a long way, thousands of miles, actually, and must speak to him now."

"He doesn't like niggers."

I fire a textbook right to his jaw, and he graciously curls onto the carpet. Mr. Davies opens the door, and I enter first. Mr. Sullivan tries to get out of bed but can't. His face is bruised and swollen, his body stiff.

"Mr. Sullivan, forgive this untimely entry, but you've been

ignoring my request for a fight."

"Get the hell outta here."

"Once we've taken care of business."

"You're a coward, coming here when I'm like this."

"You misunderstand, Mr. Sullivan. I more than anyone am concerned about your health. When you're well, we'll make each other quite rich, indeed."

"I've never fought a black man and never will."

"I've resolved, Mr. Sullivan, that we'll either fight for money before a vast audience or for free in the street."

"The latter's fine with me."

"You're not thinking clearly," says Mr. Davies.

"Perhaps a drink would help," I say.

"My doctor said no alcohol for at least two more weeks."

"The gentleman sounds like a prig," I say. "You must relax to properly heal."

Mr. Davies reopens the door, and to the fallen sentinel says, "It appears you're all right, sir. Make haste and bring us three buckets of champagne."

Jim Jeffries at the Bar

More than forty years ago right here in San Francisco at this very bar, must've been around 1904, I was drinking with some admirers when Jack Johnson strutted in and demanded I fight him for my heavyweight championship of the world. For about a minute I listened to his boasts about speed and defense and how he'd carve me up, then told him to get out before I knocked him out. Johnson persisted, what an obnoxious fellow he was, so I reached into my coat, grabbed about two grand, and slammed it on the bar and said, "Let's go down to the cellar, and this money's yours if you make it back up the stairs."

"I ain't no cellar fighter," he said, "and you're afraid of blacks."

"This way," I said, pointing the index finger of a big left hand ready to flatten him.

Johnson darted the other way, out the door. What he said's a lie and I'll show you why. Look at our records. I beat Joe Choynski at his best in 1897. The slender but savage left hooker got enough sympathy points to receive a draw after twenty rounds. Any sober observer knows I won the fight and he survived. In 1901 aging Joe stiffened young Jack Johnson with a single left high on his head, and not even Johnson would claim Joe could've ever done that to me.

And what about Hank Griffin, a good black fighter I knocked out in 1896 and battered four rounds in 1901, letting him survive so he could collect a hundred bucks. Let me tell you, Hank Griffin outboxed Jack Johnson about six weeks later to win a decision and the following year twice confused and fought him to a draw. Really, I'm glad a man weak as Johnson didn't go into that cellar with me. He'd have fallen like Bob Fitzsimmons and Jim Corbett, white heavyweight champions I knocked out twice each.

And let's take a look at Peter Jackson. Right, Jackson was about thirty-seven at the time but I'd been reading since I was a kid that this "magnificent black warrior" was the best fighter in the world, far better than the great John L. Sullivan. Thirty-seven isn't that old. Admit it. Jackson couldn't match or avoid my power, and twice I decked him in the second round and stopped him in the third.

That's the record. I fought and beat black boxers and gave Jack Johnson a chance right here. So people ask, what happened against

Johnson in 1910? By god, I'm telling you I was poisoned and don't know why I didn't understand that then but damn sure do after thinking about it forty years. There's no other way Jack Johnson could've beaten me, even when I was thirty-five and hadn't fought in six years. In training camp I lost all fat and beat hell out of sparring partners and was good as ever. But you know damn well in the fight I was dizzy and confused and weak. Now, I'm not saying Johnson was guilty. I'll give him this: he believed in himself. I'm sure some gamblers wanted to ride the long odds. They bet on Johnson and got rich.

Some whites wanted me to defend their manhood and battle Johnson again but I was sick of fighting or else wouldn't have quit the first time when I was only twenty-nine. Not many champions have the sense to do that or leave forever after that first miserable comeback.

Dancing with Jack

Don't tell my parents, at least not yet, but I've been working at Jack Johnson's beautiful nightclub in Chicago and living in an apartment with another sporting girl. I hated being a secretary. I don't love entertaining strange men but feel I have to until I get what I want and that's Jack Johnson. I've never had the feeling I get when he walks into a room. I've never danced with anyone so exciting. I've never been with a man so fine. I think that's why lots of whites are scared of him, that and his boxing.

"You should send your wife away," I tell him one night.

"Can't do that. Etta's ill."

"What's the matter?"

"She a nervous lady."

"You don't need that. You need me."

"I need the world, baby."

After Etta shoots herself in their apartment above the club, in 1912, I try to spend more time with Jack but he says, "Lucille's my girl now."

"You don't like her better than me, do you?"

"Afraid I do."

"You can't use me like that."

"That's what you're paid for."

"Fuck you, Jack Johnson."

He grabs my right wrist and twists. I think he's going to hit me like he did poor Jim Jeffries and a few girls around here, and use my left hand to go for his eyes. He easily blocks that, slaps my face, and says, "You're fired."

Stanley Ketchel Survives

Reluctantly, I accept the assignment to go back to a dreary 1910 Ozark ranch where the only woman is a plump and rough-looking cook. When Stanley Ketchel arrives for breakfast, carrying a .44 pistol, he heads for his usual chair but she offers another, and the nervous middleweight champion surveys the kitchen and places the weapon in his lap after he sits.

The cook puts Ketchel's breakfast on the table. He picks up his fork. Behind him, Walter Dipley creeps through the door, gripping a .22 rifle, and shouts, "Get your hands up."

"Drop it," I order, pushing my revolver into Dipley's back. He complies. I shoot him anyway. So does Ketchel.

"Had to do it," I say. "Far as I'm concerned, this cook is a murderer, too."

"I haven't killed anyone," she says.

"Your boyfriend was about to," I say, locking her in a closet. I open a window and shout for the ranch foreman to fetch the sheriff.

"Who are you?" Ketchel asks. He tosses a tablecloth over Dipley.

"I'm your new manager. You keep all the proceeds but do what the hell I tell you or we rewind the clock and I don't show up today, and you go home in a box they bury under a twelve-foot gravestone in your beloved Grand Rapids."

I don't see the devil who purportedly lurks in Ketchel's pretty blue gray eyes. I see a little boy.

"You're crazy."

"So long," I say. "You won't remember this."

"What do you want?"

"Only what's right. Be proud you left home at age fourteen and rode the rails like a bum before you arrived in Montana two years later and worked briefly as a bellhop until you flattened the bouncer and took his job and pounded countless unruly customers and took on all-comers for twenty bucks a week in a theater and had three hundred unofficial brawls before you became a professional and beat almost everyone until you became champion."

"You think I'm not proud?"

"I'm just setting the stage for what's gotta change. No more drinking."

"You a nun?"

"Your drinking, as much the fights, is why you're recovering here on this damn ranch."

"I'm not giving up women."

"Of course not. Just get the right ones."

"That's private."

"It is. But no more smoking opium in bed or anywhere else."

"Only done it a few times and don't like it. But the champagne…"

"Buy champagne for the ladies but never trust a lady who drinks too much."

"What a boring life."

"Better than a bullet in the lung."

"I'm still gonna drive cars fast as I can."

"Wish you wouldn't but can't make an issue of everything. I want you to have the grand house with a huge music room where friends and family can gather and sing."

"That's always been my dream."

"Then stay away from Jack Johnson."

"I know I can beat him next time."

"Bullshit. Even holding back and casually using his left he bruised your face and dominated the fight."

"But I damn near won, floored him in the twelfth with a helluva right."

"That was a lucky punch. And then what happened? You ran in, and with a single punch he knocked you colder than a mackerel. Two of your teeth stuck through your lip, and he brushed two more from his glove. Any heavyweight you beat doesn't have great skills, and I'm only going to put you against great fighters your size."

"I've already knocked out all the middleweights."

"Not the best ones."

"Who?"

"Harry Greb, Sugar Ray Robinson, Carlos Monzon, and Marvin Hagler."

"Who the hell are they?"

"The greatest middleweights ever."

"I can take 'em."

"You'll soon have a chance, three times each."

Greb and Ketchel mauled each other, delighting fans and other sadists. Ketchel got the first split decision, Greb the final two. Losers cried robbery each time. Robinson outboxed a lunging and grunting Ketchel twice but was knocked down for an eight count during the second fight, a unanimous victory for the Michigan Assassin. Monzon, more reckless than Ketchel in personal matters – he killed his wife and fatally crashed his car during a prison furlough – was the model of prudent aggression and decisively decisioned Ketchel their first two fights. The third time Ketchel penetrated Monzon's defense and rocked him once or twice a round, starting in the ninth, and satisfied all judges. Hagler pounded Ketchel their first fight, forcing uncharacteristic retreats, and won nine rounds to three. Their second encounter was the fight of the millennium, twelve rounds of sustained barbarism resembling the first round of Hagler versus Tommy Hearns. Hagler won a split decision, and both men vowed never to fight again. I wouldn't have been in Ketchel's corner, anyway, as I was jailed after my third arrest for smoking opium in a cathouse. Stanley cried when they handcuffed me in court.

"We'll pray and sing for you every night," he promised.

Battling Siki

I've got a popular speakeasy here in Hell's Kitchen. We attract plenty of characters and the biggest is Battling Siki. He went from Senegal to France as a kid and won the light heavyweight title by knocking out national hero Georges Carpentier in a fight Siki was supposed to throw but decided not to when Carpentier hit him harder than agreed.

"Those other stories about you aren't true, are they?" I ask.

"Which ones?"

"That you strolled around Paris with two Great Danes."

"They behaved. If they didn't, I fired my pistol at the sun. I really preferred African animals. I walked my lion cub on a leash but he got too big. Police made me give him to the zoo. Same with the monkey on my shoulder. Used to shit all over the apartment. The French claimed I was a disgrace. Why didn't they blame the monkey? They just didn't want a black champion."

Siki says his title was stolen by an Irishman in Dublin and he couldn't get fights in France, and I know it had to be because of his drinking, which is real bad. He usually starts off hugging everyone, even kisses some guys on the cheek, but after awhile he's frowning at the guys he kissed and, judging by the tone, cussing them in a variety of languages including English he's picking up fast.

"I'm going to beat Jack Dempsey."

Joe says, "That's why Kid Norfolk kicked your ass. We don't have weak European fighters here."

Siki slaps Joe, who falls, and leaves me a tip three times his bill.

A couple of months later Siki tells Fred, "I need big money against white fighters."

"You won't get that till you learn to beat Negroes."

Siki right hooks him to the jaw. I help Fred up and think how good guys must be to beat this muscular man.

"There'll be no more drinks for you here," I say, cautiously.

"No, please, yes." He hands me all his money. "And take my shoes and pants and shirt. Here, take my ring."

In socks and underwear he walks out and takes a taxi, and next day the driver tells me he asked Siki for the fare and the boxer said, "Pull over, I'll fight you for it."

Death in the Ring

That's not bright anywhere, especially in Hell's Kitchen. Siki needs to control himself. Boxing guys tell me he doesn't like to train and rarely runs in the morning. How could he? He's drunk about every night and often wakes up in jail. The whole neighborhood's talking about what happened in a speakeasy not far from here. Siki told a guy, "I'd be heavyweight champ if I was white."

"You're a bloated light heavyweight loser," the guy said.

Siki slugged him, picked up a stool, brained the approaching bartender, and fired the stool into the mirror behind the bar.

Next time I see Siki, he's got a bunch of stitches closing knife wounds in his face.

"Louis," I say, "That's your real name, right? I read it in the paper. You've got a wife here. And a lady and a son back in Paris. I'm telling you straight, you better stop all this stuff so you can take care of them."

"I have no children," he says.

"And I have no booze for you."

Thankfully, he hasn't been drinking. He starts that somewhere else. Two policemen later see him staggering along the street. "You want us to arrest you?"

"No thanks, I'm fine."

Battling Siki stumbles on. He's heading for his apartment. I imagine he feels pretty bad. He may not feel the pop. It hits him in the back. He keeps walking. There's another pop but he still keeps moving. He'll get home. He's on his belly now, crawling in the gutter. He's crawling in Hell's Kitchen.

Sam Langford Today

I understand the logic but am still offended by friends and others who've often said, "Sam, you're too short for football and basketball and not fast enough afoot to compensate."

"Compensate for what?" I ask the dear fellows. I made all conference in both sports at my prep school and I'm starting at defensive back for my university, a place in Cambridge that produces more presidents than gridiron heroes.

"But you could be a world champion," they say. "In fraternity sparring sessions you decked Dave with an uppercut, broke Joe's jaw with a left hook, fractured Frank's nose with a right cross, and cracked Charlie's ribs on both sides. Nobody hits like that."

That may be correct but is irrelevant since those I'd be fighting, at the highest level, would hit me often and sufficiently hard to damage my mental and physical health. I presume you've seen Ali and Frazier and the Quarry brothers and Chacon and Robinson and other walking dead. I especially hope you've seen the first Sam Langford. No thank you. I don't want to again become a blind beggar, groping for a warm spot, after a legendary career highlighted by countless wars and infinite punches in gyms and arenas. As if by sledgehammers my nose was flattened, my lips shredded, my eyes lacerated, my strong body beaten into early convalescence, and my social nature pounded into passivity. I don't want to sacrifice that to beat you up. Indeed, I don't want to strike you at all. Besides, I've determined sparring disrupts my golf swing.

I'm Harry Greb

Damn that Kid Norfolk. I know he thumbed me before I thumbed him. Now I can barely see from my right eye.

"I'd rather die than quit," I tell my wife, Mildred.

"Let the doctor help you."

I go to the hospital and he puts patches on both eyes and says wait a week in bed. It's hell, even when Mildred's here. I pray to leave this darkness and get my sight back and am about crazy the day the doctor takes off the patch over my left eye.

"It's still fine, Doc."

Then he removes the patch over my right.

"This one's good, too."

"You're blind on this side."

"No, I can see great."

He covers my left eye with a paper and asks, "How many fingers am I holding up?"

"Three."

"I'm not holding up any, Harry."

"Please don't tell anyone. Promise me."

"What if you lose the left eye?"

"I won't. I guarantee it."

I'm the best in the world. At opening bells I charge across rings throwing left hooks, right hooks, uppercuts, jabs, bolo punches, punches you haven't seen from angles you never imagined at speeds opponents can't match. I'm the Pittsburgh Windmill who fights every week or two. I pound Gene Tunney. I pummel middleweights. I beat light heavies. I outbox heavyweights. But I can't stop tuberculosis from taking Mildred in 1923.

I'll fight for her. A few months later I win the middleweight title and earn plenty of money for our daughter and thank my sister for taking care of her when I'm on the road. I'm lonely out there and lucky to meet Noemi. She's beautiful and loves to laugh with me.

Maybe I should retire. Gene Tunney beats me pretty bad in 1925 but he's now the best heavyweight in the world and I know will handle Dempsey. In July I almost knock out young slugger Mickey Walker while defending my middleweight title. I still have most of my ability and the following year don't know why Tiger Flowers, a long and smooth left hander, gets my title by decision many think I earn and then keeps it next time when I clearly win.

"Unless that right eye comes out, you'll probably lose the other one, too," the doctor says.

"All right, Doc, just put something in there that looks nice."

My eye hurts like hell even though it's gone and the socket's worse especially after some fool leaves a wagon in the road. I swerve and roll my car and bust a bunch of bones in my nose.

"You'll get better, sweetheart," Noemi says.

"I'm dizzy and my head's killing me and so's my eye and everything else and I know I'm gonna die."

"Let's go to the hospital."

I don't like hospitals so we go to a clinic where the doctor tells us, "All you need is a local anesthetic, and I'll pull those broken bones right out."

Fifteen minutes into the operation it seems like the local isn't enough and they're rushing to give me other things.

Tiger Flowers at the Wheel

"Don't you drive that roadster so fast," says Willie May.

"It only goes fast as the Lord wants it to."

I never do anything without first asking Him. He's the one who made me quicker than Harry Greb and let me circle and dance and move in and out and smack Mr. Greb most every time he tried to grab and hold and roughhouse, and I thank Him for the middleweight title and thousands of my people who welcome me in Atlanta and carry me like a prize to one of many cars that ease through our part of town.

Okay, I'm by myself and out in the open now and push the accelerator and feel real good moving twenty miles an hour, thirty, fifty, sixty, eighty, ninety, a hundred and more. Okay. Better slow down. I don't want to tempt the Lord. I go back home. It's a villa built on ten lots and has big windows and lots of rooms for Willie May and our daughter and many friends.

My wife often says, "Don't get comfortable, Theodore. You've got to keep fighting. We need a lot more money to maintain this home, and that we cannot do unless you work and buy more houses for us to rent."

"I love this place but no more than modest places we've lived."

"We're not gong back, Theodore."

After the referee raises the hand of my punching bag, Mickey Walker, I promise the Lord, and Willie May and my manager Walk Miller, that I'll get the title back. I'll fight often. I fight nineteen times in 1927.

"Maybe I better slow down, Mr. Miller. I'm thirty-two and had a hundred sixty fights. I can hardly breathe through my nose. Remember what happened to Mr. Greb."

"He had three hundred fights and wasn't nearly as fresh as you. You'll get a rest after surgery."

In the clinic Mr. Miller receives a call from Walker's manager promising Walker will soon sign for a rematch.

"Our future's better than ever," he says.

I take off my boxing robe and say, "Please put my bible under the pillow. And if I should die before I wake, I pray thee, Lord, my soul to take."

Jack Delaney on the Rocks

I don't like boxing and neither do my lady friends but we love Jack Delaney who's about the handsomest man in the world. His thick brown hair is perfect. His eyes are bright and gorgeous. His nose is classic and still straight. His mouth is sexy. His body's lean and muscular. We love gathering at his fights, with thousands of other ladies, and cheering our romantic hero. The New York press calls us Jack Delaney's Screaming Mamies.

All of us dream about him. Imagine being married to a man who moves around the ring like a dancer, jabbing and hooking to confuse opponents before knocking them out with smooth right crosses. Once in a while Jack loses but almost always wins and even becomes light heavyweight champion in 1927. I decide I've got to try to meet him. I call around and find out where he's training for his next fight. I thought he trained in New York or maybe Bridgeport where he lives but find out he's training way out in the country.

I take a bus there and am so excited. There he is, beautiful brown and boxing outdoors, and he smiles and winks at me, and when he's finished sparring says, "I'm tired of camp, like jail around here."

His manager and trainer frown and say, "Beat it," but Jack tells me where to wait and I do and that afternoon we jump in his car and drive to a train station where he buys two tickets for New York City. In the dining car we have a drink and Jack finishes his in about a minute and orders another and we're having a great time though he worries me drinking so much and talking louder and drinking even faster. I swear he has at least ten drinks the first hour and tells the waiter, "Keep em comin, for the lady, too."

"No thanks."

"That's okay, I'll drink yours too."

"Slow down," says the waiter.

"You hurry up."

Two porters come back with the waiter and Jack stands and knocks one down with a right cross and the other two men jump on him and he pushes the waiter off and wrestles the porter down the aisle, and the man keeps his head tucked into Jack's stomach until Jack pushes him against the wall and fires a right the porter ducks, and Jack shouts, "Oh, Jesus," and strokes his right hand with his left.

In New York the police threaten to arrest Jack but he says, "My damn hand's broken and I've got another big fight."

"Then you better head back to camp," says an officer.

Jack puts his left arm around me and says, "Let's do the town tonight."

"No thanks," I say, but give him my telephone number.

I hope he'll call and pray those rumors aren't true he does this all the time. I wait months then decide I better not go to any more fights. I'm really glad I miss his 1928 match with Jack Sharkey. Our Jack Delaney, according to the ladies, shows up flabby and in a daze and after opening bell doesn't throw a single punch and just lets Sharkey knock him to the canvas where he crawls around maybe looking for the next drink.

Mickey Walker on Canvas

I loved pounding people, especially with my left hook, and winning the world welterweight and middleweight titles, and would've continued fighting if I hadn't gotten older and lost six times in two years to guys who probably tended bar. I kept drinking like a champion but started every morning feeling like I'd been knocked out and decided to quit.

Geez, what a change. I'm interested in culture and watch a movie about Gauguin and think that's what I want. I want to paint like a champ. But maybe I can't. I'll find out. I head to the art supplies store and warn the kid not to say anything about me buying all this stuff. What am I worried about? I get hooked right away and have a helluva time.

"Mickey. Do you hear me?" asks my wife.

"Yeah, yeah."

"Am I bothering you?"

"Yeah."

"You're painting fifteen hours a day, sometimes more."

"Wish I had more energy."

"For your mistress."

She repeats that in divorce court. Fine. I've already married three women a total of six times. Can't worry about them. I've got canvases to fill. Look at these, I tell everybody I see. Are those guys joking about offering me an exhibition at a big hotel? Experts call me primitive but that's not necessarily bad in painting. I feel scenes and know what colors and moods are necessary. People buy quite a few of my works. Amazing. There's something better than sex, booze, and boxing.

Top Thirteen Heavyweight Champions

For a century heavyweight boxing champions were the kings of sports, the baddest men on earth, and celebrities of the first rank. In the last twenty years, however, after the in and out of ring demise of Mike Tyson and the emergence of mixed martial arts as a more comprehensive and less destructive form of fighting, the heavyweight crown has been placed on a dresser in the rear bedroom and its holders have become as obscure as utility outfielders. Let us set aside recent history and recall the days of more gifted and charismatic champions. Here are the thirteen best of all time.

13. Ken Norton – The former marine with a sculpted physique forever placed his name in the fistic pantheon by hammering Muhammad Ali in three fights. During the first bout, in March 1973, Norton broke Ali's jaw, repeatedly hurling his strong roundhouse right, and won a split decision that one myopic judge gave to Ali. I attended their next fight, in September that year in Los Angeles, and watched Ali, as he'd sadly begun doing, spend too much time on the ropes and get clobbered. Unlike in their first fight, though, Ali sometimes punched authoritatively and won a disputed split decision. About that, legendary Los Angeles Times columnist Jim Murray wrote, and I paraphrase only a bit if at all: "If Ali won that fight then Japan won World War II."

In his next bout Norton was destroyed by George Foreman in the second round but then stopped seven straight opponents before meeting Ali again, in 1976. Norton was more aggressive as Ali masochistically leaned against the ropes, again, but also slow danced and scored enough to make it close at the bell when Norton screamed, "I beat you. I beat you." Judges sympathetic to Ali unanimously disagreed with Norton who wept in the ring. The fairest way to assess their three fights is to say Norton at minimum fought Ali to a draw and probably had an edge.

12. & 11. Wladimir Klitschko and Vitali Klitschko – The Klitschko brothers loom too large and talented to be kept out of the top tier any longer. Both men are knockout punchers and excellent boxers. Vitali is especially adroit in the ring, holding both hands low as he stands just out of range, like the young Ali, waiting for the

instant to strike smaller opponents. He also has a formidable jaw. Wladimir doesn't take punches as well but that deficiency has become less problematic as he's learned to use his size to keep dangerous punchers out of range before he demolishes them with one of the best overhand rights in boxing history. Who's better, Vitali or Wladamir? The brothers don't want to think about it, and ceased sparring with each other in the early nineties. I applaud their fraternal restraint but, as an exercise in fantasy, would bet on the more rugged and resourceful Vitali over his bionic brother.

10. Jack Johnson – The Galveston Giant had more trouble battling white supremacists than boxers in the ring. He dominated a series of opponents for several years while title holders, promoters, and politicians connived to deny him a championship fight. In 1908, when Johnson was thirty years old, the establishment couldn't say no anymore, and he journeyed to Australia to batter wee Tommy Burns and claim the crown. Johnson was a great boxer and defensive stylist and good power puncher who, once he reached his prime, beat everyone until, as an overweight drinker and world traveler at age thirty-seven, he tired under the Cuban sun and was nailed on the jaw by young giant Jess Willard.

9. Sonny Liston – His name still evokes images of a glowering ex-convict who used extremely long and powerful arms to chop down more than three dozen opponents, in particular the popular but much smaller Floyd Patterson while winning the title by first round knockout. He dispatched Patterson the same way in a rematch. After that he in 1964 prepared to fight young and rambunctious Cassius Clay, who in part appeared to be as afraid of him as other opponents but also called him ugly and a bear and said he was going to whip him. Clay at age twenty-two was and remains the quickest heavyweight ever, and his lateral movement and jabs and overhand rights befuddled and bruised Liston who retired after the sixth round with a strained shoulder. In their rematch Muhammad Ali, as he'd changed his name and religion, threw a right that may have landed but certainly not with force sufficient to pole-axe the sturdy Liston, who refused to get up. The two debacles against Ali should not diminish Liston's historical standing. Every man has a nemesis, and most have several. Sonny Liston flat kicked most people's asses. He had less success with personal demons, and died

of a heroin overdose in 1970.

8. & 7. Mike Tyson and Evander Holyfield – In the mid-1980s a five-ten teenager began his career throwing combinations with the speed of a lightweight and the power of a sledgehammer, stopping his first nineteen opponents and delighting TV sports news watchers in a pre-internet era. At age twenty he flattened Trevor Berbick to become the youngest heavyweight champion, and many said no one in history could have survived against him. Like all fighters, however, he proved to have vulnerabilities. When Tyson was twenty-three, before a nearly-silent crowd of boxing neophytes in Tokyo, James "Buster" Douglas popped the champion with long left jabs and strong straight rights, dominated the fight if not two of the three scorecards, survived a Tyson uppercut to arise at the count of nine in round eight, and in the tenth delivered a pulverizing uppercut and several more punches that left the champion on the canvas as he groped for a mouthpiece he shoved partially into his mouth while being counted out.

At age twenty-five Tyson was convicted of rape and served three years in prison. After his release he beat several overmatched foes before Evander Holyfield defeated him by technical knockout and won their rematch as a frustrated Tyson twice bit Holyfield's ears. The glory years never returned for Mike Tyson but no fan will forget his spectacular rise.

Superbly conditioned Evander Holyfield, who also beat a prime Riddick Bowe once in three ties and Lennox Lewis in the second fight – forget the absurd decision – must also be placed among the fistic immortals. He punched hard with both hands, adroitly blocked blows with his arms and hands, moved well, and was exceptionally competitive.

6. Joe Frazier – As with Ken Norton and Sonny Liston, this fighter's name will always be linked to that of Muhammad Ali, who before their first fight, in 1971, repeatedly badgered Frazier and called him ugly. Ali should have remembered that after a three-and-a-half year banishment from boxing, for refusing to join the army during the war with Viet Nam, he no longer "floated like a butterfly and stung like a bee." He'd become a heavier, often flat-footed fighter who tragically concluded, starting with this fight, that the best way to tire out a supremely-conditioned opponent was to let him use Ali's

head and torso as a heavy bag. Frazier relentlessly obliged, ripping countless left hooks – the finest in boxing history – into Ali's body and the right side of his face. Ali had begun the fight decisively, battering Frazier's head with combinations, but Smokin' Joe got stronger, or weakened less, and staggered Ali a couple of times and ensured victory by flooring him with another explosive left hook in the fifteenth and final round. Joe Frazier won a unanimous decision but it was a Pyrrhic victory, as it would have been for Ali. Both men had to be hospitalized, Frazier even longer than Ali, and it's certain their brains suffered permanent damage.

Two years later Frazier was bombarded from his title by George Foreman and then lost a nontitle decision to Ali as the latter moved more adroitly than in their first fight, and both men escaped major beatings. In their third meeting, the Thrilla in Manila in 1975, the titans bludgeoned each other for fourteen riveting rounds that culminated with Ali knocking Frazier's bloody mouthpiece onto the canvas and continuing with power punches that rendered Joe unable to come out for the final round. The real outcome of the fight: Ali, once the world's most dynamic talker and entertainer, has been silent nearly thirty years, and Frazier garbled his words for several years before his premature death in 2011.

5. Joe Louis – Like Muhammad Ali a generation later, Louis was even more important as an inspiration than fighter. During an era when blacks were segregated and had no vote and couldn't live or work where they wanted, the Brown Bomber showed them they could overcome. If they worked hard enough, they could be like Joe Louis. They could knock the man on his ass. That's what Joe Louis did better than anyone until George Foreman. During an unprecedented twelve years as heavyweight champion, he put people on the canvas with short, pulverizing combinations, and listeners huddled around their radios, waiting for thunder.

The most celebrated fight of Joe Louis was his second against Max Schmeling. In 1936 the former heavyweight champion and a German, though not a Nazi, had clipped Louis on the chin with his best punch, an overhand right, dropping him in the fourth round. Louis later said he didn't remember anything the rest of the fight, which lasted until he was knocked out in the twelfth round. Two years later, an angry and focused and more mature Louis unleashed one of the most horrific one-round beatings in ring annals, registering a tangible victory over Der Max and a symbolic one over fascism and racism.

4. George Foreman – At age nineteen, during the 1968 Summer Olympics in Mexico City, Foreman established that he wielded a left jab like most boxers' power punch and a right hand that immediately weakened strong men. He launched his professional career with a string of victories, most by knockout, and in January 1973 went to Jamaica to challenge the heavyweight champion, Smokin' Joe Frazier, the undefeated conqueror of Muhammad and a man believed to be unstoppable. Foreman knocked Frazier down three times in the first round and three again in the second, some of his punches lifting Frazier from the canvas. This remains the most overwhelming display of knockout power on record. I watched this fight live on closed circuit at a theater in Sacramento.

The new champion soon stopped Ken Norton in the second round and, based on his demolitions of Frazier and Norton, the only two fighters who'd beaten Ali, he seemed certain to knock out the challenger. The fight was staged in Kinshasa, Zaire (now Congo) and billed "The Rumble in the Jungle." Ali again used his "rope-a-dope" tactics, his back on the ropes and arms a shield from elbows in his stomach to gloves over his face. Though incomparably powerful, Foreman was exposed as a slow puncher and Ali repeatedly dodged the champion's gloves, pushed him around, and nailed him with sharp punches. Suddenly, in round eight, Ali sprang from the ropes and hit a tiring Foreman on the jaw with the best overhand right of his career, and the mammoth champion folded at the waist and hit the canvas and was unable to rise. From my seat in Sacramento's aged Memorial Auditorium, I stood in homage.

In his next fight Foreman and ex-convict Ron Lyle repeatedly staggered and knocked each other down in a brutal and exciting fight. (Big matches were sometimes still on TV.) Foreman stopped Lyle in the fifth round, but the years of lopsided wins had ended. In 1977 slick boxer Jimmy Young outmaneuvered Foreman, floored him in the final round, and earned a unanimous decision. Foreman, only twenty-eight years old, stunned boxing fans by retiring. Many assumed this farewell, like most in boxing, would be brief. It wasn't.

Ten years later Foreman made a comeback, which seemed a

preposterous act. He was not only old for a boxer and long inactive but carried forty pounds more than in his prime. Many spectators and sportswriters sneered at the flabby and sometimes clumsy former champion. Foreman ignored them and again started knocking people out and after winning twenty-four straight fights, all but one by stoppage, he at age forty-one faced Evander Holyfield for the heavyweight title. Holyfield moved and punched too quickly for the ponderous challenger, and after Foreman's loss by unanimous decision most observers assumed he would permanently retire. Instead, he continued and won three fights before losing a decision to Tommy Morrison, a good but not stellar fighter. The setback somehow led, more than a year later, to a title fight with undefeated Michael Moorer. For ten rounds the forty-five-year old Foreman was pounded by the quick and strong Moorer. Watching on pay per view in my Bakersfield living room, I simply wanted the fight, and the old man's career, to be over. Then, suddenly, as if summoning magic from his younger self, Foreman landed a straight right that hurt Moorer, and a couple of seconds later unloaded an even harder right that knocked Moorer out and made George Foreman by far the oldest heavyweight champion in history.

3. Lennox Lewis – Lewis will never be forgiven for two things: he dominated most of his opponents and failed to inspire while so doing. Even his sometime trainer Emanuel Steward publicly rebuked him for, in effect, settling for safety while winning decisions instead of risking himself to score bloody knockouts. Lewis nevertheless stopped his opponents seventy-two percent of the time, one of the best rates among heavyweight champions, and possessed an authoritative right hand. In a career lasting fourteen years Lewis lost only twice and later reversed both with knockout victories. He beat many notable fighters, including Evander Holyfield, Mike Tyson, and Vitali Klitschko, behaved in a gentlemanly way, and will likely lead a longer and healthier life than most former boxers.

2. Larry Holmes – Holmes was the physical equal of Muhammad Ali but tormented that he lacked the loquacious one's charm and charisma. He shouldn't have worried. He controlled fights with the finest left jab in boxing history and frequently ended them with terrific right hands. Like Lennox Lewis, he rarely had the opportunity to fight great boxers in their prime, so his dominance

was frequently either ignored or misunderstood. Holmes won the title in a stirring 1978 battle with Ken Norton. He pummeled Norton early before the latter gained the advantage, and the outcome was determined in the fifteenth round when the men planted themselves and flailed each other until the bell. It was a split decision, and the last close fight Holmes would have for several years. In 1985 he was fairly outpointed by Michael Spinks, who became the first standing light heavyweight champion to capture the heavyweight crown. Holmes surely won the rematch, though the split decision was awarded to Spinks. He retired for two years before joining the assembly line of Mike Tyson knockout victims. That loss is no more relevant to his career standing than old Ali's loss to Holmes or aging Tyson's final two losses to guys few remember.

1. Muhammad Ali – Ali began his career as quick and elusive Cassius Clay who was as entertaining before and after fights as when pummeling less gifted opponents. After his three and a half year exile Ali fought much differently, flat footed and trying to exhaust opponents by letting them hit him. The greatest defensive stylist became the best at eating bombs without falling. He won many epic fights and faced more quality opponents than anyone in boxing history. He fought five people on this list of special champions a total of ten times and also twice defeated two-time champion Floyd Patterson as well as numerous other distinguished fighters such as Oscar Bonavena, childhood sparring partner Jimmy Ellis, Jerry Quarry, Earnie Shavers, and Leon Spinks, in a rematch after squandering his title in the first fight, his back again needlessly on the ropes.

After his succession of wars in the 1970s, Ali lost his ability to speak, and those from subsequent generations, unless they've studied videos online, have no concept how compelling he was. He made people believe in him and inspired them to believe in themselves, and he campaigned for civil rights and human rights and urged people to question political leaders who lied and waged unnecessary wars, and he still personifies bravery and good humor as he battles Parkinson's disease and other maladies. He was and shall remain "The Greatest."

Death in the Ring

Cowboy Luttrell Demolishes Jack Dempsey

Editorial Note: Descendents of rugged wrestler Cowboy Luttrell recently published this startling letter, which two handwriting experts have verified the Cowboy authored. We're searching Jack Dempsey's archives and will publish anything on this subject certifiably written by the Manassa Mauler.

To Whom It May Concern:

After he poorly refereed my tag team match in 1940 I pushed Jack Dempsey and challenged him to wrestle but he insisted we put on gloves and have a regular match several weeks later. I'd done some boxing as a kid and was twenty pounds heavier and ten years younger than Dempsey so figured I could rough him up but at opening bell he charged and hit me with left hooks and a rabbit right and more lefts and I covered up before eating many combinations including some nasty uppercuts. Pretty soon I couldn't move much and another left staggered me into the ropes at end of round one.

I'm a tough cowboy and attacked Dempsey to start the second round but caught a right cross to the jaw and more of those damn lefts to the head. Go ahead, keep hitting, I told Dempsey. You can't hurt Cowboy Luttrell. Dempsey replied with more two-fisted head shots and knocked me down once, twice, three times. Referee Nat Fleischer, the boxing editor who was a worse referee than Dempsey, must have enjoyed the slaughter and didn't stop it, and I was too game to ask and too dumb to stay down. I was slumped against the ropes – where was Fleischer? – when Dempsey stepped in and uncorked a left uppercut that launched me out of the ring. Okay, I got my face taped up in the dressing room and acknowledged boxing was Dempsey's game.

Several months later, when most of the damn bruises had healed or lightened, I drove to New York City and stormed into Jack Dempsey's restaurant. He walked up, hand extended, and I ducked and drove my head into his balls, wrapped my arms around his knees, and bulled him onto the floor where I sat on him and punched down a lot harder than he could punch up and was busting him pretty good when some of his goons pounced and hit me from behind and dragged me outside. Come on, I motioned to Dempsey, let's finish this on the sidewalk. He waved me off. In a real fight, he knew Cowboy Luttrell was tougher.

Sincerely,

Cowboy Luttrell

Death in the Ring

Straight Punches by Jack Dempsey

Editorial note: We weren't optimistic we'd find any Jack Dempsey missives about Cowboy Luttrell, but the great granddaughter of one of Jack's four former wives emailed a photocopy of his 1941 letter in response to Luttrell's boast that he'd trounced the Manassa Mauler in his Manhattan eatery. Dempsey's letter was published in the New York Amsterdam News, an African American enterprise that had often criticized him for refusing to face black fighters.

Dear Fans,

I'm not going to waste much breath on Cowboy Luttrell because I slaughtered him in the ring and knocked him flying out of it. He's not only a lousy boxer and flabby wrestler, he's a liar. He came into my restaurant, all right, drunk as hell, and cursed and challenged me but this time I didn't have to deck him because he swung and missed by a mile and collapsed face down. I booted his butt and my boys carried him out.

Maybe I shouldn't have looked so sharp last year when I fought Cowboy in Atlanta. Thousands of fans had greeted me with fantasies when I got to town, thousands more came to the fight, and many more later got excited by the newsreel shown in theaters around the country. Come on back, Jack, everyone said. And I agreed. I felt I had it again. I even said it'll take a guy with great power in two hands to beat Joe Louis, and that guy could be Jack Dempsey. If everyone had been as easy as Cowboy I might have continued to believe that. A couple of months later, though, some wrestler got me in a headlock and damn near squeezed my eyes out. It didn't matter I eventually knocked him out with a shot to the gut.

I also noticed Jack Johnson, age sixty-one, was publicly challenging me but avoiding Joe Louis. I'd knock out either Johnson or Louis in my prime, for sure. You've got to feel that way or you're not a fighter. Look at Jess Willard flatten Johnson and then how I crush Willard's face. And see Max Schmeling knock out young Joe Louis. I'd have stopped Der Max in a round or two. Yes, I know a more experienced Louis tenderized Max awhile ago. We can debate who'd have won when we were at our best. Right now, though, we all know I don't really want young Joe Louis, and Jack Johnson doesn't really want me at age forty-five. What we all crave is to forever be heavyweight champion of the world.

Sincerely,

Jack Dempsey

Death in the Ring

Jack Johnson Challenges Dempsey

This 1941 column by former heavyweight champion Jack Johnson was published in The New York Times *in response to public boasts by Jack Dempsey.*

That's right, folks, my robust opinions are in *The Times* while the Manassa Mauler has to moan in the obscure *Amsterdam News*. How appropriate. For years I pursued frightened opponents around the world before winning the heavyweight championship at age thirty. Jack Dempsey got his title young and spent the next seven years dodging formidable black fighters, pummeling white stiffs, and fooling around in Hollywood. I don't begrudge him the latter, but when a man's most significant victories come over hundred-ten-pound starlets, he's no champ, at least in the ring. And, please, disregard those who say I was bad as Dempsey in denying black fighters opportunities. I only did that after I became champ. At least I fought my brothers while I ascended.

Study the record. Jack Dempsey, already a lazy titleholder, didn't fight for three years before skinny Gene Tunney peppered him ten rounds. Dempsey was then an old man at thirty-one. At that stage I kept getting better. That's why, if Dempsey had given me a shot in 1919, when I was only forty-one, I'd have boxed and confused him and made him stumble around the ring before I dropped the hammer. But of course Jack Dempsey wouldn't fight me then. Maybe he will now. I'm sixty-three and been losing most of my fights for years.

Joe Louis also irritates me. I don't know why black folks cheer such an inarticulate guy. They must not remember. If I were twenty-five years younger, I'd tattoo the Brown Bomber. You think Max Schmeling would've knocked me out?

George Thomas Clark

Joe Louis Rebuffs Jack Johnson

This handwritten note by Joe Louis was released by his estate last week.

Jack Johnson, after decades of boasting and white-womanizing and running from the law, thought he was going to bring his fat old ass into my championship camp and take center stage. I told Johnson what my people told him: get the hell away from us. We don't like your style, we don't like your mouth, we don't want your problems and you're not going to give us any. When he realized he was back on the street, Johnson began calling me Uncle Tom and saying I had a glass jaw and he'd have killed me. I would've given him the Schmeling treatment if he'd been around. I really didn't need to, though. People on Harlem streets more than once punched him for insulting me. I loved hearing that.

Unlike Johnson I wanted a clean image. And I had one. I kind of kept it, too, but some people found out I occasionally roughed up women including Lena Horne. I wasn't that kind of guy. It wasn't my fault. It was all those punches. My head hurt and wasn't working right, especially after years of snorting cocaine. Don't try that. My nose is on fire all the way to my head and my head knows they're coming to get me. I won't let them. I'm blocking the door. I'm covering the windows. I'm sealing the vents. I've got to get away. Please help. Let me shake hands in Las Vegas. People in casinos still call me champ. But I'm not planning a comeback. I'm in a wheelchair.

Dashing Dempsey

Ed's a fan of Jack Dempsey and believes the hundred-eighty-seven pounder would've thrashed larger and more skillful boxers Muhammad Ali and Larry Holmes and outslugged powerful George Foreman. I disagree with Ed's boxing assessments but appreciate he's a discerning reader who emailed that he'd recently seen a baseball documentary and the former champ, filmed waving to fans, projected "incredible charisma" and his girlfriend Sally liked his looks.

"Great," I replied. "Please ask her to call me for an interview."

She dutifully responded.

"I hear you dig Dempsey."

"I thought he was dapper and quite handsome for a guy getting hit in the face," Sally said. "He also had a nice smile."

"So, if you'd lived then, would you have gone after him?"

"I wouldn't have been interested. I don't like violent people. We probably don't have enough in common."

"Ed was pretty violent, a high school wrestler and college football player."

"He was also valedictorian of his law school class. IQ is essential to me."

"You shouldn't assume Dempsey was dumb," I said. "He ran a large and successful restaurant."

"I'm speaking in general. I wouldn't have sat ringside and tried to look cute for him."

"I'm disappointed. I was hoping for something lascivious."

"Boxers always have really pretty girls, but what are you going to talk about with most of them? I was a trophy girl, too, but always wanted educated guys."

I thanked Sally for her comments and asked to speak to Ed.

"Is she really that straight?" I inquired.

"Now, sure. You should've asked thirty years ago."

George Thomas Clark

The Dempsey Obsession

In recent weeks I've been writing columns some of which imply that white Americans still obsessively overestimate the boxing prowess of Jack Dempsey. Yes, he was swift and hard-punching, by century-old standards, but to be honest one must ask: who in the hell of note did Jack Dempsey ever beat? The answer is: no one remotely as good as Muhammad Ali's most distinguished victims: Sonny Liston, Joe Frazier, George Foreman, Ken Norton, Floyd Patterson, Jerry Quarry, and Earnie Shavers. Let's be specific about Dempsey's reign as champion: after beating a plodding and inert target – Jess Willard – to win the title, he over the next seven years defeated Billy Miske, Bill Brennan, Georges Carpentier, Jimmy Darcy, Tommy Gibbons, and Luis Angel Firpo, all of whom would've been overwhelmed by the Ali opponents listed above, and numerous other Ali foes. If you're not conversant with boxing, you may be stunned that Jack Dempsey, as champion, never fought a black boxer.

Dempsey fanatics are appalled by such statements. One commentator called me Eldridge Cleaver, a strange remark, and another wrote that Dempsey would've demolished Ali because Frazier "beat the hell out of Ali" in their first fight. In a boxing sense, so what? Ali also battered Frazier, and Frazier had to be sequestered in the hospital a long time. The men in fact destroyed each other's health that 1971 night. The mutual damage was even worse in the 1975 Thrilla in Manila. Dempsey, at any stage of his career, would've been thrashed by either man, both of whom were quicker, stronger, and better boxers than the Manassa Mauler.

It must also be emphasized Ali had a three and a half year layoff, six months longer than Dempsey's. Inactivity certainly hurt both fighters. Yet, when both were age thirty-two, in 1927 and 1974, respectively, an inept Dempsey was carved up by Gene Tunney, while Ali knocked out George Foremen. No one else ever did. Foreman would've pounded Dempsey like a heavy bag.

Why not tell the truth? Jack Dempsey was a charismatic and exciting man who hit (generally undistinguished) opponents hard, and, more importantly, helped (and continues to help) whites convince themselves that they aren't generally inferior to African American athletes. A lot of whites evidently don't watch football, basketball, and track. And they shouldn't start. The reality would be too painful, and we'd have to listen to their fantasies of Red Grange dominating the NFL and George Mikan dunking over Wilt Chamberlain.

Marciano Dines at Dempsey's

Jack Dempsey extended a thick hand, shook another, and said, "Welcome Rocky. Come on." The former heavyweight champions strolled through Dempsey's busy restaurant, greeting patrons, and briefly stopped to sign autographs before moving into a private room. They both received chicken, mixed vegetables, and protein drinks confidentially prepared.

"This is serious business, Rock."

"Sure is."

"I'm happy to be young again but don't know if I want to box."

"That's the only way they'll let us stay," said Marciano.

"Who's they?"

"Don't know but it doesn't matter."

"We've more than proved ourselves," Dempsey said.

"Not against the Klitschko brothers."

"They don't take much of a sock. I'd bust their chins."

"Could be, Jack, but maybe not at your usual one-eighty-seven. I've accepted I'll have to put on at least twenty to two-oh-seven or so, to take out guys six-six and two-forty-five. I think you could comfortably carry two-seventeen."

"I see Evander Holyfield's lifting weights a lot. They're okay but I don't want to do too many, and certainly not all that damn jumping and twisting and walking on hands, while a guy carries his feet, that Holyfield does."

"We were workers, Jack. This could be exciting. Holyfield was only about our size, now he's got thirty pounds more muscle."

"Well, he did kick Tyson's ass. Suppose he wouldn't have without all that strange stuff."

"What's Gene Tunney gonna do?" Marciano asked.

"We talked but he's happy paling with Shakespeare and George Bernard Shaw."

"Ali's going along with this. I talked to Angelo Dundee, and he sees his guy weighing two-thirty and being fast as he was at age twenty-two."

"Rock, I was born before the automobile and airplane, and I sure use them now. I'll go along. But I won't fight you. Just those two big Russians."

"I think they're from Ukraine."

"Same thing," Dempsey said. "They've got beautiful bodies but can't take what we'll give 'em."

Wladamir Klitschko Versus the Legends

Alternating between German, Russian, and Ukrainian, I recently talked to Wladimir Klitschko at a lavish European spa and learned that while his brother, Vitali, concentrates on becoming president of Ukraine, he, Wladimir, the younger behemoth, is accelerating preparations for Jack Dempsey, Rocky Marciano, and Muhammad Ali and honored they consider him so formidable they've revised diets and training routines and rebuilt their physiques. Wladimir encouraged them to keep improving. He's tired of dominating dreary contemporaries and yearns for the glory of crushing three legends in fights soon to be held.

"How will you deal with Dempsey?" I asked. "He now weighs a rippling two-twenty and, according to everyone he's hitting, his left hook is devastating and the right almost as dangerous."

"Respectfully, Dempsey is still too small for me," said Wladimir. "I'm several inches taller and twenty-five pounds heavier. He won't be able to penetrate my defense. I'll feed him jabs and drop nuclear right hands on his head."

"That you may well do, Wladimir, but wars are seldom so neat and predictable. There's a reasonable chance that Dempsey, who's demonstrably quicker than you, will charge inside and rake your ribs, as well as your chin, with power punches. And we should remember that you've been stopped three times. Corrie Sanders and Lamon Brewster revealed your chin isn't unusually sturdy."

"That was a decade ago and, if I may borrow one of your adverbs, I'm demonstrably better now."

"Your second fight is against Marciano. He was the strongest hundred-eighty-seven pounder in boxing history, and now is probably the strongest at two-oh-nine."

"He should've dropped to cruiserweight. I've got an enormous reach advantage and will be punching down while he's crouching and trying to approach. I expect him to go down early. I acknowledge I'll probably have to deck him a few times. I think this fight will resemble the Foreman-Frazier matchups. One guy's just too big. No disrespect to the Rock, who may beat everyone else, if he decides to continue."

"Your third fight will generate the world's first billion dollar gate

– The Greatest versus the renowned Dr. Steelhammer. Ali's biologically twenty-three years old, quicker than he was against Liston, and about sixteen pounds heavier at two-twenty-eight. Remember, many believe even the lighter Ali could've beaten you. He's difficult to hit, has a punishing jab and right cross, and, unlike you, has shown he can get off the deck and fight coherently. Also, at this weight he'll be hard to put down."

"I agree with some of your assessments. He has an iron head and great defense. I'm probably not going to stop him. I'll instead shoot my right hand into his mouth and make him wish he was fighting a tall skinny guy like Ernie Terrell rather than a scientific brute."

"He's fought many top fighters and is more resourceful than you," I said. "I think that's the difference."

"I'll wager ten million."

"Dollars or Euros?"

Gene Tunney Returns

I see Jack Dempsey thinks Shakespeare and I have been hobnobbing in literary heaven. Actually, the truth is rather more mundane. I've been competing against experienced thespians, outperforming the louts, and am scheduled to debut as Hamlet, but restrictive political and economic circumstances as well as dreadful sanitation in early seventeenth century England have compelled me to accept a hundred million guarantee to reclaim my youth and career as an undefeated pugilist dedicated to deflating the engorged prima donnas of today.

My instincts urge me to retain my former physique and fight as what's now called cruiserweight, a division in which I'd be nigh on invincible. Who could compete? If any of the many current cruiser champs wants to find out, he must immediately move into the heavyweight division since as before I've resolved to become the ultimate champion, even in its current dimension. I therefore accept the new standards of nutrition and training and establish a target weight. Standing six-feet and spanning seventy-six inches, I feel two-hundred-ten muscular pounds, twenty more than before, are prudent.

To my most ardent critics – generally those who never fought me – I say that my already authoritative punching, which produced forty-eight knockouts, will be enhanced by additional long and lean muscle, and that my unsurpassed boxing skills will make me difficult to hit. Look at the films. I bounced and moved and fired as well as the young Ali. This style developed quite naturally in the physical sense, and also accorded with my conviction that only unwise men stand and trade with fellows who hit just as hard. Thus, at propitious moments I slid in, unloaded, and glided away.

Please do not interpret my confidence as arrogance. I am a prudent man who took risks only after contemplation. For Jack Dempsey, I formulated a plan years before we first fought. I perceived that he could be hit by right hands, but I bore a chronically sore knuckle. On a 1920 afternoon as I rode the ferry toward my hometown, New York City, I noticed the broad frame of new and celebrated champion Mr. Dempsey. I marched over and introduced myself as a campaigning professional, still rather slender, and was greeted warmly so told the champ about my ailment. Instantly, in two huge gentle paws he took my injured right and examined the swollen knuckle, rubbing it carefully, and advised me to add extra tape to the right and left of the distended knuckle, thus diverting energy of impact into padded areas. I followed instructions, and also fought regularly while the champion celebrated in London, Paris, and Los Angeles. After 1923 he failed to fight for three years. I meanwhile added weight and muscle. Then I twice tattooed Mr. Dempsey.

Today, using legal scientific means, I may accelerate the weight gain, but I shan't debut against Tyson or Ali or Foreman or Louis or either Klitschko. I'll first take on two top thirty current heavyweights, then two top twenties, and ultimately two top tens before I drive the first spike into Mt. Rushmore. At this time, with all luminaries receiving nine-figure bonuses, I cannot promise who I'll first fight. But, in confidence, I can reveal a few of my tactical plans.

Against Tyson I assuredly won't stand and trade. I'll jab and move and nail him with the overhand right that, after our first fight, Dempsey said he never really recovered from. Mr. Tyson is a grand fighter. If I err, I'll fall. Danger I'll avoid by being forever cautious, except when aggression is needed. Then I'll fire rapid rights and lefts. I do not believe this powerful young man will see my punches, which are fast as any those of any middleweight. Whatever Tyson sees earlier he'll be blind to later. Top drawer stamina is not among his many gifts.

I'm intrigued by Wladimir Klitschko and not inclined to delude myself he's another Jess Willard or Primo Carnera. No, Mr. Klitschko is a modern beast, superbly conditioned, alarmingly muscular, and skilled as a boxer. Against this gentleman I will frequently dance outside his reach, which at eighty-one inches is not terribly greater than my own, and when he throws his long and admittedly quick punches, I'll dodge or duck and shoot inside to pound his body and lash his head, and then disappear until I punish him again. He'll get tired. He'll get frustrated. He won't catch me. He'll catch more leather.

No sane man could underestimate George Foreman who, to my eyes – forget the scale – is bigger and stronger than either Klitschko. I shan't charge him and be bounced around like Joe Frazier. I shan't freeze like a Ken Norton deer in headlights. I'll make Mr. Foreman work. He'll work to pursue me. He'll work as I slip his pile-driving left jabs. He'll tire as I dodge or block his sweeping rights. He'll first flinch and later stumble as I pummel him with right crosses and left hooks. I've seen his Jimmy Young fight thirty times. I've seen his Tommy Morrison fight at least twenty. Don't you think I can do what those guys did?

I'm James Joseph Tunney, friend of Shakespeare and other Muses, but you may call me Gene as I blister Messrs. Tyson, W. Klitschko, and Foreman. And then I sense I'm going to fence with Ali. He's a kindred warrior. So is Larry Holmes. But I won't presume to fight Holmes. That's the duty of young Ali, to avenge the wounds inflicted on his elder self. Thus, Ali and I will be the final survivors as this high-tech war climaxes. I believe the world will watch.

Vitali Klitschko Thinks

I'm my brother's most ardent supporter and he's mine, otherwise we'd have long ago determined the king of the Klitschkos. Really, we view ourselves as what we in fact are: the two unchallenged monarchs of a still-renowned heavyweight division. Americans are missing our great long-running show, and I must respectfully ask: what's the matter, USA, don't you have any big guys who can fight? I've heard the response: sure we do, but most are in the NFL. That's a convenient analysis. I'll confine myself to reality.

I must start with Corrie Sanders, a fine fellow who died trying to save loved ones from bandits at a wedding in South Africa. Corrie was a hell of a hard puncher, had a terrific overhand left. I was angry and hurt when he repeatedly bounced Wladimir off the canvas. Thankfully, I faced Sanders his next fight, ate the same shots Wladamir did, withstood them well, and over eight rounds battered Sanders, launching long jabs and right crosses leading to more head-rattling rights until the referee saved him. My victory was for Wladimir, whose chin has improved.

A number of fistic legends have challenged me. And I graciously accept. Contrary to what many Americans charge, I'm not hiding in Europe. I'm the champ awaiting qualified challengers. Are they willing to come? If they do, I'll handle Jack Dempsey and Rocky Marciano like two tough but very little boys. They'll absorb five or ten punches for every one they land, and please don't tell me guys loads lighter are somehow stronger. If do they beef up, as threatened, I'll simply hit them a few more times.

A two-hundred-twenty pound Joe Louis, I confess, worries me. I've studied his combinations, and they're perhaps the best in boxing annals: fast, accurate, and powerful. I'll defuse him by using the Max Schmeling guideline and bombing the Brown Bomber with right hands. And my long left, which Der Max did not possess, will prevent Louis from regularly penetrating my defense. I'm so fine I'll stop him in nine. Ali emailed me that one.

I know I'm not knocking out Ali, and neither are you. He takes a punch better and recuperates and counterattacks more effectively than anyone in the history of this sport. He survived some bombs from George Foreman before knocking him out. He could've fallen many times in his first and third Joe Frazier fights but persevered and stopped Joe late in their finale. Against Earnie Shavers he caught some frightful right hands yet recovered and was staggering Shavers at the final bell. Those who say Ali can't punch need to dine on a few of his rights preceded by cutting left jabs. Having thus praised him, I can forthrightly say Ali isn't going to stop me, either. We're going to jab each other, and I'll be first more often, and we'll trade rights, mine being more frequent and powerful. To those who say Ali's a more fluid and resourceful fighter, I respond: we'll see.

For my last ring skirmish I want Lennox Lewis. The first time I was beating him until he busted me over the eye. Admittedly, this was the thirty-seven-year old's last fight and I was in my physical prime. Maybe I'll toughen my skin with some of Dempsey's brine. I'll have to. Lennox Lewis and Muhammad Ali are two of the four best ever. Wladimir and I plan to complete the quartet.

Adopting Sonny Liston

For fifteen years my wife Ellen and I, Memphis educators both, tried hard to have a child. Our failure to conceive was alternately attributed, by purported experts, to my sterility and her barrenness. Perhaps both reports were correct. We did not argue. We decided to adopt. Paperwork and prejudice at local agencies compelled us on a summer afternoon in 1935 to drive into eastern Arkansas where, in St. Francis County, we quite accidentally pulled onto wretched land marred by a shack in front of which a stocky and rather aged sharecropper used a long stick to whip the back of a young boy.

Out of my car I bounded to demand, "Stop this at once."

"Want some, too?"

"No, sir, I believe I'd like to give the boy a decent home."

"Take him. Had twelve by my first wife and thirteen by thisun. Don't need so many kids."

"Tobe," yelled a much younger woman. "Sonny's not leavin."

"You've been threatenin to leave for years, so when you do I'll be takin care of the boy."

His mother hugged Sonny, whose back was scarred well as bleeding from fresh wounds, and I approached and whispered, "Please, let the boy have a chance. You can visit whenever you want. I promise."

Crying, she nodded.

"How old's the boy?" Ellen asked.

"Probably about seven."

"Sonny's his given name?"

"It's Charles," she said.

"Charles, you're going to have a new home," I said, and he rode home between my wife and me. We worked out the legalities with the Listons soon as we could.

That fall Charles, who couldn't read the alphabet, had to start in first grade. My wife and I not merely helped him with homework, we read stories to him, we showed him pictures in the newspaper, we took him to church, we entertained and were hosted by other families, we encouraged him to play games outside with nice boys in our middle-class neighborhood of negro professionals.

In less than two years Charles was reading at his age level and moved up to the appropriate grade. Ellen and I were relieved, and for more than academic reasons. The boy was growing fast. At age thirteen he was bigger and stronger than most men. Like all boys, he got into occasional scraps but we disciplined him: no play time for a couple of days and five hundred word essays. He hated those but wrote pretty well. His mother, Betty, visited twice and seemed happy for her boy before she took some of her kids and moved to St. Louis.

In high school Charles maintained a B average, starred on the baseball and football teams, and dreamed of being a professional. We said there weren't any like us. Some roughneck adults tried to convince him to box, said a youngster so strong, with bulging arms, could win a fortune. We always ran them off. Our son was going to college, Tennessee State, our alma mater.

Charles earned good grades in college but sometimes got drunk at parties and beat guys up. We'd heard alcoholism ran in the Liston family.

"Charles, please don't drink," we urged him. "Accept you can't handle it."

"I'll try, Mom and Dad, I promise."

Sonny is Santa Claus

Look at this, my father said, showing my mother, sister, and me the December 1963 cover of *Esquire* magazine. This is the greatest Santa Claus ever.

"I didn't know Santa was black, dear."

"He is now, and I've hired him to attend our corporate Christmas party next week."

"He's cute," said my sister, age five.

"That's Sonny Liston, meanest man in the world," I said.

I'd recently stopped believing in Santa and replaced him in my pantheon of heroes with athletes, especially Mickey Mantle and Floyd Patterson. Sonny's first-round demolitions of Floyd last year and this had frightened me. My father knew Patterson casually and had rooted for him but was always a businessman attuned to opportunity. "Sales at the firm are down," he told my mother before looking seriously at my sister and me. "And, damn it, President Kennedy's just been assassinated. We need a lift and so do my employees."

Normally, children didn't attend corporate functions but this year there were as many kids as adults, and chatter by young ones filled the ballroom. "When's Santa Claus coming?" they kept asking. This Santa, it developed, came when he wanted, about an hour late. And he was dressed in slacks and a sports shirt. Two men in suits accompanied him.

My father dashed up, as I eagerly followed, and said, "Sonny, Mr. Liston, you're supposed to be dressed as Santa Claus," and handed him a cap like he wore on *Esquire's* cover.

Sonny extended Herculean arms and pulled the red and white cap over my father's head just above the eyes. He walked to a table, turned a seat around facing the crowd, sat down, and started talking to kids. He had a great smile. I still think in person Sonny had the best smile I've seen.

The Santa believers first gravitated to Sonny, who held them on his lap and asked their names and what they wanted for Christmas. When the kids said tricycles, bicycles, baseball gloves and bats, and various toys, Sonny said, "I'll see what I can do. You're gonna be good, aren't you? Where are mom and dad?"

When the kids pointed, Sonny looked pleasantly at them and

asked, "Santa can do that, can't he?"

I know my sister got her red tricycle and can confirm several other kids got what they requested. Sonny was a great Santa Claus. And after that night I couldn't imagine him having all those problems. I believe things would've been better if he'd always drunk orange juice as he did with us.

Visiting Sonny Liston

Heat already dominates a Las Vegas morning punctuated by jets soaring west into the heavens. On the opposite side of Eastern Avenue there's another heavenly place: Davis Memorial Park. Rather than enter the business office and risk receiving an earthbound commitment to protect a man's privacy, I wave to a maintenance man driving a tractor. He stops, and I say, "I'd like to pay my respects to a champion."

"Follow me, I'll show you where he is," the man says, and drives to a cemetery road running parallel to Eastern. He hops off his tractor, marches east across cut grass, and in twenty seconds we're there. "Thanks," I say, looking at a simple sun-damaged nameplate:

Charles "Sonny" Liston
1932-1970
'A Man'

About half the gravesites in the cemetery have flowers in metallic vases. No flowers emerge from the vase of Sonny Liston. I reach inside and find a small white plastic flower attached to a green wire stem. A miniature United States flag is planted nearby.

George Thomas Clark – Excuse me, Sonny. May I please talk to you?

Sonny Liston – About what?

GTC – Boxing.

SL – Only boxing. You understand?

GTC – All right. Sonny, you had a great record. Have you decided to participate in the Heavyweight Legends Boxing Tournament?

Sonny Liston – Doubt it. I'm tired of fightin, tired of gettin hit.

GTC – Maybe you'd be motivated if you were twenty-five and had all the competition and money and excitement.

SL – You like gettin punched in the face at twenty-five?

GTC – No, but I thought…

SL – You thought here's this big so and so happy gettin hit in the head.

GTC – I just thought you loved to box. And that you'd like a shot at Dempsey or Marciano or a third shot at Ali, then maybe the Klitschko brothers.

SL – I'd kick Dempsey's ass. He'd look like a lightweight next to me. Same for Marciano. Now the Klitschkos are big boys. I'd need ten rounds to chop 'em down. But not on the same night.

GTC – So you're willing to fight 'em on consecutive nights.

SL – Don't get smart ass. Every boxer respect his opponents, no matter what he say. I always liked to look mean because didn't know how to look any other way, 'cept with kids and my wife. I scared hell out of opponents and that made 'em easier to hit.

GTC – Both Klitschkos, as you noted, are quite tall and muscular. And they have good long jabs and powerful right crosses, the same punches Ali hurt you with.

SL – You said I'd be twenty-five, not the thirty-six or who the hell know what I was second time I fought Clay. Don't forget, I got a few inches reach on both Klitschkos, and I got the hardest jab in history. I'd be the one pushin my fist through faces.

They've never fought anyone tough as Cleveland "Big Cat" Williams. Knocked him out twice in the fifties. He was in his prime then. Clay got Williams after the police shot him in the gut. He lost a kidney, had a withered left leg.

GTC – What happened in those two fights with Ali?

SL – Just told you. I got too old for a young guy who turned out better than everyone thought. His jab was quicker than mine, so was his right. And his feet…never seen a heavyweight move like that.

GTC – Could you have gotten up after the knockdown in the first round of the second fight?

SL – What the hell for?

GTC – Was that really a knockdown?

SL – Think I'll show you how it felt.

Babe Ruth v. King Tut

I mustn't take credit for this fistic revelation. No, I never would've imagined if a profound historian hadn't commented that Babe Ruth and King Tut fought in 1929, and he, the scholar, resented reading stories by those who were not there. Few of us active today could've been cognizant that year, so, at the risk of angering our historian, we must confer with the internet to first confirm the fight did indeed take place and learn how such a remarkable matchup came to be and who won.

Astonishingly, the online footprints are in many places evident, though they were not released until a few hours ago, and both film clips and written testimony certify that young King Tut did indeed battle The Babe inside the ropes. How did a fellow born more than three thousand years earlier take on anyone in 1929? It was all elementary. King Tut, mummified by tape-like material similar to that protecting the hands of pugilists, was marvelously preserved and, by enhanced cloning, readily brought alive into the Roaring Twenties.

Having solved the once-unimaginable shift in time, the facilitator faced an even more overwhelming problem. He beheld a slender lad of no more than nineteen who was weakened by genetic mischief: his parents were brother and sister and left him with a congenital limp and other imperfections. How, indeed, would the facilitator prepare such a fellow to box Babe Ruth?

First, he enlisted an elite orthopedic surgeon to reconstruct King Tut's hip. Then he called Jack Dempsey, who at times had exercised with the often corpulent Ruth and knew his capabilities and weaknesses better than any boxing man. Dempsey, retired since being twice dissected by Gene Tunney, in 1926 and 1927, was anxious to prevent the still-swatting Babe from overtaking him as the premiere athlete of the twenties, and at once agreed to privately tutor young King Tut, who was generally sequestered or, when glimpsed, said to be a welterweight from Cairo. Ruth was aggrieved Dempsey had declined to handle him and vowed to take on the ex-champ after he demolished his opponent.

We must credit Dempsey for teaching King Tut to box scientifically, like Gene Tunney, and praise the lad for bravery: even after months of eating steaks and training fiercely he never scaled more than a hundred fifty rather frail pounds. He and Dempsey were at least encouraged that Babe packed about a hundred more and, rather than train, daily consumed whiskey, cigars, and women. He was being tutored by Shakespearean scholar Tunney who, let us admit, was becoming no small drinker himself, and was at any rate not invested in the well-being of his unlettered slugger.

The fight itself, as you've surely concluded, could not take place publicly and would instead draw revenue from film distribution. King Tut, though not blessed with formidable muscles, proved adept at shuffling left and right and retreating, and possessed fine reflexes enabling him to duck all of Ruth's power punches, which were either slow left crosses or slower left roundhouses. Tut did not bang but occasionally jabbed his tiring foe in the nose. By the start of the fifth round everyone knew Babe Ruth would not go the six-round distance. He'd need a knockout. And for that he'd need skates. King Tut shuffled and slid along the canvas like Hans Brinker on ice, and after another Ruthian windmill left missed, the king unleashed his only right of the fight, straight to Babe's chin, and he dropped to a knee and puffed as he took a ten count that could've extended to thirty.

This dustup remained secret since King Tut soon expired, Ruth didn't want to be embarrassed, Dempsey and Tunney were gentleman, and facilitator Al Capone, concerned about taxes, vowed to kiss anyone who squealed before today.

Mandela v. Obama

The two young legal wizards of Johannesburg, Nelson Mandela and Barack Obama, became rivals upon their first handshake when the right-handed Mandela squeezed Obama's hand until the latter sighed: "Oh." Obama, a southpaw, immediately demanded a re-shake, with left hands, and Mandela squeezed and pulled him down to one knee. Obama popped up, shoved Mandela two-handed on the shoulders, and said, "I'll see you in the gym."

This confrontation could've been precipitated numerous other times when the attorneys, in behalf of clients, battled each other in divorce cases and civil suits, and, most portentously, for the leadership of the anti-apartheid movement in South Africa. Those seeking liberation had delectable options: both men were handsome, charismatic, and committed. Ordinarily, two such talents don't peak at the same time, but no movement can have co-leaders. One would have to be chosen.

Many constituents suggested a vote. Mandela and Obama, though proponents of democracy, dismissed this approach as unworkable since the other would likely stuff ballot boxes. No evidence indicated either man had such nefarious intentions, but their mutual antipathy and distrust had become toxic, and they agreed on but one premise: the winner of their boxing match two months hence would carry the flag of liberation.

Betting at once favored Mandela, a natural heavyweight who carried about two hundred pounds. Obama, born to be a light heavyweight, weighed around one hundred eighty, and suggested the weight limit should be one-ninety.

"This is ten rounds for the heavyweight championship of South African politics," Mandela told reporters. "If Mr. Obama feels that's out of his league, I quite agree and offer my condolences."

Obama began drinking much milk and doubled his intake of beef. He also quit playing basketball, which had consumed two-thirds of his time in the gym, and three hours daily sparred and hit the heavy and speeds bags. Mandela was pure boxer and occasionally remarked that throwing a ball through a hoop was immeasurably less relevant than knocking down a man who's trying to hit you.

The South African government announced that whites would

not be allowed to attend the event, and fight promoter Steve Biko said, "Sorry to hear that. We had a special 'Whites Only' section prepared in the upper deck."

By fight day, at the weigh-in, no one was talking much about politics. Reporters stressed that Obama, freed from dashing up and down a basketball court, had strengthened himself and now weighed a hundred eighty-four, fifteen less than muscular Mandela who said, "Obama can consume all the cows he wants. He's still skinny."

At fight time, as referee Joe Louis gave instructions before ten thousand chanting fans, Nelson Mandela and Barack Obama tilted their jaws up and stared at each other until Louis told them to shake hands. They declined to do so.

At the bell Mandela rushed across the ring and threw a lead right that the already-moving Obama avoided and countered with an overhand left that hit Mandela in the forehead and evoked a smile. "Hope you have a bit more than that, Barack."

"I won't find out what you've got."

Mandela may have considered this sage advice – don't insist on trying to hit a swift southpaw in the head – and began pounding Obama's ribs, two lefts and a right and a left and two more rights. This downstairs bombardment characterized rounds two, three, and four, and in the fifth Obama, who had stopped moving much, planted himself in ring center and several times feinted right jabs and landed left crosses that amused Mandela. "Barack's like those light heavies you fought, right, Joe?"

In seconds Obama absorbed several sturdy left hooks to the jaw and a right that sliced a two-inch gash above his left eye. Joe Louis waved strong arms overhead and called in the doctor who said, "That's it."

Death in the Ring

Heavyweight Scholars at War

It was only a teaser, that's all it was, the video and article on a boxing website about actor Rip Torn hammering would-be thespian Norman Mailer on his crown and thereafter grappling with the bloodied writer as the latter's wife cursed Torn and his children cried to cease hostilities. The august site of online pugilistic discourse, I must tell you, was withholding the most sensational parts of the story, a story we all should've learned about and cherished a few weeks ago. I assume the website's fact checkers and attorneys are mired in bureaucratic quicksand, but my investigators decidedly are not, and this is what they've just revealed: there was an incomparable martial tournament titled Heavyweight Scholars at War, and it involved not only Mailer and Torn in a rematch sans hammer, but William F. Buckley versus Noam Chomsky, Gore Vidal against Truman Capote, and Ernest Hemingway, finally, toe to toe with William Faulkner. All fights would last a maximum of one five-minute round, the winners would clash a week later, and the two finalists a week after that. Results would be immortalized by crystalline video.

Hemingway and Faulkner never met in life and thus spared themselves much squirming. For this confrontation they requested to be themselves at age thirty. Upon entering the ring, and one should know it was actually an octagon and all that implies, Faulkner smirked at Hemingway, said his syntax was infantile though better than anyone else's save that of the Oxford sage, and suggested they chug moonshine rather than joust. Hemingway, who outweighed Faulkner by at least fifty pounds and always lusted to fight men much smaller or older or both, head butted "old corn-drinking mellifluous," as he occasionally called his literary rival, flattening the master of inscrutability and pouncing on his inert frame, big ass on Faulkner's chest and knees pinioning him on either side, and unleashed four or five haymakers before the referee, a huge man, administered a naked choke from the rear and pulled Hemingway off.

Truman Capote and Gore Vidal next entered the octagon. Capote had selected age twenty-three, Vidal twenty-nine. The cautious warriors circled each other for two hiss-inducing minutes before Capote shot at Vidal's left leg and, unable to lift it for a takedown instead released his left hand and, from his knees, unleashed a mighty uppercut to Vidal's insufficiently-padded groin. Vidal howled and collapsed to the canvas and the unimpeded Capote sprang to his feet and thrice kicked him in the head until the redoubtable referee military-pressed Capote and said, "It's all over."

William F. Buckley and Noam Chomsky each wanted to be twenty-five. Buckley the cold warrior attacked Chomsky the pacifist, pounding air as the acrobatic Chomsky ducked and danced. Chomsky in fact threw not a single punch while Buckley unleashed two hundred, at least, but landed only a few on Chomsky's forearms and shoulders. Near the end of the fight relentless Buckley windmilled a wild left, an errant Curtis LeMay bomb, that propelled B-52 Bill onto the ground whereupon Chomsky placed his gloves on either side of the slugger's head, and William F. Buckley tapped out.

"Had to, or that communist would've choked me into incontinence," he said.

"I was simply trying to assist the gentleman to his feet," stated Chomsky, ever the contrarian.

Epic though these three battles were, they played no larger than a barroom dustup in the hearts of spectators who wanted the biggie, the new World War II, Norman Mailer versus Rip Torn.

Mailer insisted on maintaining the forty-seven-year old physique he brought to his first clash with Torn. Torn said fine, he'd stay the same he was, thirty-nine. "This fight will not be determined by chronology," Mailer declared, "it will hinge on existential angst," a quote he attributed to Jess Willard.

In fact, Mailer was overanalyzing something rather more elementary. That's why he'd begun writing novels fourteen hundred pages weighing several kilos.

As the referee administered instructions, Mailer examined Torn's hands and said, "Without your Pearl-Harbor hammer, what're you gonna do?"

"I shall mesmerize you prior to Armageddon."

Mailer began the bout timidly, pawing with his left jab and sending rights several inches short of Torn's jaw. After the fifth insufficient right Torn countered with a left hook, nailing Mailer's jaw, and followed with a tackle putting him on top of Mailer on his back, as in their cinematic clash. Mailer alternately grabbed Torn's biceps and wrists to preempt punches. When Torn, astride his horizontal foe, began winding up to punch down, Mailer steadily used heels and buttocks to pull himself under Torn and spin to hands and knees and then to his feet.

Arms akimbo, Torn circled Mailer, contorting his face, earnestly saying indecipherable things, impersonating Charles Manson loaded on exceptionally strong acid. Grunting and cursing, Mailer moved in, left jabbing, right crossing, and left hooking, usually missing, never landing solidly on Torn's quick-moving head. Torn scored another stinging left hook and again took Mailer down and sat on him and threw shorter punches, landing quite a few, and Mailer screamed, "I'm going to cold cock you," and Torn drove his right elbow into Mailer's nose, which splattered, and fired several more punches before the big referee pulled him off and raised his hand.

I was bummed but hoped Hemingway, despite his gargantuan drinking and eating, and athletic self-delusion, would trounce the cat-eyed Torn. I did worry Papa had decided to come in a little soft at age thirty. Rip Torn, even at thirty-nine, was much tauter, and boxed and moved in the style of Gene Tunney. Every time Hemingway charged, Torn gored him with jabs and crosses and, occasionally, with jolting left hooks. After four minutes, hyperventilating and bleeding from nose and mouth, he stumbled onto the canvas where Torn pounced and choked him out.

Noam Chomsky and Truman Capote, vocal ringside commentators before the fight, at once issued a join statement of retirement and denounced everyone in the tournament as a warmonger.

George Thomas Clark

Knockouts

Another Knockout by Archie Moore

On a summer evening in 1980 I called Archie Moore, introduced myself as a correspondent, stated my admiration for his thunderous punching, and asked for an interview while he was in Sacramento to be honored during an amateur boxing tournament.

"That's fine," he said. "Can you come about eight tomorrow morning?"

"Well, is ten or eleven okay?"

"No, I'll be busy later. I'm free at eight."

"Sorry. I can't come then."

In the most mellifluous voice I've heard, he asked, "Whhyy?"

Had I been candid, I'd have answered, "I usually work till midnight and then stay out too late and struggle to get up at eleven or so and even then often feel like a zombie." Instead, I said, "Ah, eight o'clock is…it's really early and I don't know…okay, I'll see you at eight."

"My room number's…"

Despite maintaining discipline that Friday night, I was frightened by the six-thirty alarm but stumbled out of bed and, in honor of a champion, did a few exercises before showering and driving to the motel. I knocked on the appointed door and waited about a minute before knocking again. Slowly the door opened to reveal the distinguished brown face, highlighted by a graying mustache and goatee, of Archie Moore, attired in a white bath towel around his waist.

"Come in, Mr. Clark," he said, and I shook his hand, noting it was much larger and stronger than mine.

Moore dressed, and for two hours I listened to boxing tales that spanned Jack Dempsey to Muhammad Ali, and when I wasn't scribbling notes a tournament official photographed us in several boxing poses that show a beanpole squaring off against a champion. He retrieved a copy of his autobiography, *Any Boy Can*, signed it and wrote his telephone number, telling me to call him when I'd next be near his home in San Diego. We then walked to the motel restaurant, where men recognized and praised him and introduced him to their families, and enjoyed a high-cholesterol breakfast he paid for. I continued jotting ideas.

After covering the boxing tournament that Saturday night, and delivering some fact-clotted words on deadline, I had my chance to perform Sunday night. And in three hours, for twenty bucks that also covered the interview time, I wrote a feature that's here revised and updated:

Rocky Marciano was hit with a right uppercut and plunged head down to the canvas, landing in haphazard fashion on his hands and one knee. He arose at the count of four and staggered into the ropes where he draped his arms while staring glassy-eyed into the crowd of sixty thousand at Yankee Stadium. Archie Moore, the forty-two-year old light heavyweight champion, tried to heed his corner's cry, "Hit him, hit him," and lunged at the dazed heavyweight titlist. But referee Harry Kessler, either forgetting or ignoring the agreement to wave the mandatory eight-count rule, jumped in front of Moore and told him to back off and started the count again. Then Kessler grabbed Marciano's gloves and jerked him in an apparent effort at revival.

That was in 1955 but Moore remains incensed. Scowling while he recalled the incident, he told me to hold my hands out to represent Marciano's gloves. He then demonstrated Kessler's maneuver with a tug that indicated "The Old Mongoose" is still powerful.

"Henry Kessler jobbed me by not letting me get to Marciano in that second round, and I defy him to prove otherwise," Moore said. "The next day, when we studied the films, it proved my case. Then, several days later, the sequence where Kessler got between us had been carefully edited out.

"I got too angry after that and started to go after Marciano. We traded a lot, and I'm convinced that no fighter, past or present, would be smart to stand and trade punches with Rocky Marciano. He decked me twice in the sixth round and stopped me in the ninth."

So Moore was unable to realize the then unachieved goal of a light heavyweight champion winning the heavyweight crown. But he owns boxing's counterpart to the home run record, that of most knockouts: one hundred forty. He was a consummate strategist who conceived countless methods to render his opponents unconscious.

"I had knockout power everywhere," said Moore. "I had no preference whatever which type of punch I hit a man with, or where.

Death in the Ring

You've just go to go, that's all. My philosophy was to get guys on queer street right away and keep them there."

Poverty, the spawning ground of most boxers, was the keynote of Moore's youth in St. Louis. He and his friends couldn't play golf or tennis so they fought bare-knuckled in the street or carried boxing gloves with them as they roamed and sought to test themselves. Those impromptu brawls in the ghettos served as Moore's amateur career.

"I didn't box in the amateurs because I wasn't interested in trinkets. I wanted money," he said, and began to fight for pay as a welterweight in 1936. His age at the time, as today, has been kept secret. The Encyclopedia of Boxing lists his year of birth as 1913. Moore won't confirm that but does admit to "being up in years."

For the next sixteen years Moore fought for subsistence wages in a succession of smoky gyms, auditoriums, and warehouses. Sometimes he earned enough for transportation to fights in the next backwater towns. Sometimes he didn't. When broke, Moore often hitched rides on freight trains and fought for the short end of purses against hometown foes favored by corrupt judges. As Moore's knockout record expanded, he had increasing difficulty convincing highly-ranked boxers to fight him.

"I couldn't get a title shot in any division I was in on the way up," he said. "Billy Conn never would fight me. Some people said I was too good for my own good. Also, I wouldn't cater to people. Did people ask me to throw fights? I don't use that kind of language, but it was tantamount to that."

In 1952, when Moore was probably thirty-nine years old, he was awarded a long-denied chance at the light heavyweight title and defeated Joey Maxim. What he had striven so long to achieve, he was unwilling to relinquish. The master of the knockout, even in his forties, was superior to his youthful competition. No light heavyweight ever beat Moore in a title fight and he retired with his championship belt in 1962.

If a man can beat the world's best in middle age and last a few rounds with much younger and larger Cassius Clay – as Moore did at forty-nine – then it's likely he'll be formidable in old age. In 1976, as an effervescent sixty-three-year old, Moore went to Nigeria to coach boxing. One morning he was being chauffeured through a scenic region outside Lagos and asked the driver to stop on a bridge so he could take a picture of the river that flowed underneath. He saw workers below who were called "sand hogs" and carried hundred-fifty-pound buckets of sand up the banks to be used in making cement. Moore was impressed with their huge, sculpted muscles, and snapped several photos. As he was returning to the car, the largest worker approached and angrily said, "Bring it."

"Bring what?" said Moore.

"The camera," said the hulking young man.

"What for?"

"I don't want you taking pictures and making fun of us."

"I'm not making fun of you. I'm your brother."

"Bring it here," shouted the man, who began to approach Moore.

The old champ's geniality had been strained. He gently tossed his camera into the car and waited as the powerful laborer charged. Moore caught the African with a left hook that knocked him against the railing and opened a bloody cut on his mouth. Still, he attacked Moore again, grabbing him around the neck.

"I could just feel that man's strength about to crush me," said Moore. "I knocked off one of his arms with my right hand and followed with a left hook to the body and a three-punch flurry. Ah, that man was so big and beautiful. He was bigger than Ken Norton. He just sank to the ground like he was sitting down."

Archie Moore had just recorded his hundred-forty-first knockout.

Editorial notes: Online footage of the Moore-Marciano fight does not accord with Archie's claim he almost knocked out the heavyweight champion. Indeed, Marciano arose right away and appeared to be unhurt. The images do not appear to be edited.

For many years Archie Moore continued to travel and regale his fans with fistic tales. I regret that I never called him and thus squandered an opportunity for more history and entertainment. Moore died in his adopted hometown, San Diego, in 1998 when he was about eighty-five.

Art Aragon's Sweetest Ladies

Hey, in the 1950s I owned L.A., had the town to myself, maybe shared it a little with the Rams. Not to brag, but I was one of the best looking guys around, better than most actors whose girlfriends I plugged whenever I wanted. I really wasn't Arrogant Art, though. I just enjoyed looking down on opponents. You gotta be tough in the ring. I should've been born later. I'd have been junior welterweight champ, guaranteed. But it was either lightweight at a hundred thirty-five pounds or welterweight at one-forty-seven. I had to squeeze my balls to make the former or battle bigger boxers in the latter. Still, I knocked out sixty-two guys.

Fans packed my headline shows at the Olympic Auditorium. Most booed me. But I guarantee some also wanted me to win, especially wives and girlfriends who'd suddenly become interested in the manly art. Lots of guys didn't like that. What could they do? If they messed with me in a bar or on the street, and that includes giving the wrong look, I'd kick ass. An occasional arrest didn't bother me. Neither did court. But it got expensive. Most of the time I was fighting to pay lawyers and former wives.

I really should've been champion. Here's what I mean. In 1951, strong and lively at one-forty-two, I decisioned lightweight champ Jimmy Carter in a nontitle fight. Less than three months later, starving and sweating myself to make one-thirty-five, I wobbled around the ring, getting dominated by the same guy. I don't know what the hell I was thinking in 1958 when I put on soft weight and fought Carmen Basilio, a brawler who'd been welterweight and middleweight champ and recently split decisions with Sugar Ray Robinson. Carmen pummeled me for eight rounds.

Less than two years later I quit, dizzy all the time. Try getting belted in the head for a living. I won't lie. Boxing's a terrible sport. I preferred being with broads. Can't give you the whole list. Space limits us. But I'll tell you I dated Marilyn Monroe and Jayne Mansfield. Imagine those two.

George Thomas Clark

Wild Life of Oscar Bonavena

Many years ago, in the 1970's, my Uncle Bob, who owned part of a casino in downtown Reno and heard many unpleasant stories, told me Argentine boxer Oscar Bonavena, renowned for brawn and feared for instability, sometimes got drunk in local bars and slapped men to the floor where he held and tormented them, spewing crude English in their faces. I recall being disgusted anyone, particularly a heavyweight contender, would behave that way, and thinking people like that don't last long.

Life as an adult had begun with great promise for Oscar Bonavena. In early 1964, as a precocious fighter of twenty-one, he debuted professionally in the palace of professional boxing, Madison Square Garden, a stage closed to most boxers even after years of combat. Bonavena won by technical knock out in the first round, fought in the Garden five times that year, and captured all eight matches in 1964, seven by knock out. Boxing fans were excited by the handsome and charming brawler, who carried huge muscles and more than two hundred pounds on a sculpted six-foot frame, and offered him many opportunities for recreation between fights in New York City. Read about Bonavena and the most common characterization is "partier." The big puncher from Argentina was also a heavy hitter with booze, and while his opponents and sparring partners pounded his head – albeit less than he pounded theirs – alcohol also battered his brain.

In his first fight of 1965, Bonavena stepped in against a larger and more experienced opponent, Zora Folley, and lost every round but one. He thereupon returned to Argentina and poleaxed nine undistinguished foes as well as decisioned the talented Gregorio Peralta to take the heavyweight championship of Argentina. Fighters don't sacrifice for titles like that. They dream of winning world championships. Pursuant to that, Bonavena returned to Madison Square Garden in June 1966 and decisioned George Chuvalo, the iron-jaw Canadian. Three months later, also in the Garden, he took on young Joe Frazier, who had but eleven professional fights and was recognized primarily as the 1964 Olympic heavyweight boxing gold medalist. In the second round Bonavena knocked Frazier down with a quick overhand right and, after Frazier scrambled up and bored in, quickly floored him again. A third knockdown in that round would have ended the fight but Frazier kept moving in and survived. In subsequent rounds he pressured Bonavena who responded aggressively, and the men pounded each other for ten rounds after which Frazier was awarded a split decision. This fight was noteworthy because only thunderous George Foreman would ever knock Joe Frazier down again, and pleasant to view since both boxers were young and healthy, unlike the battered warriors they became, and Frazier spoke clearly and good-naturedly in the post-fight interview. Years later he rambled and was difficult to understand.

In 1967 Muhammad Ali refused to join the army and kill Vietnamese whom he emphasized had never called him "nigger." His title was then stolen by a self-righteous and warlike establishment, and the World Boxing Association set up a tournament to determine the ersatz champion. As a high-ranking heavyweight, Oscar Bonavena went to Germany in September and confronted Karl Mildenberger, the decided favorite based on his impressive losing performance against Ali, and knocked the German down four times en route to a unanimous decision. That December, Bonavena was one fight removed from his coveted title opportunity, but Jimmy Ellis, Ali's childhood friend and training partner from Louisville, twice decked the Argentine while winning the decision and advancing in the tournament.

Oscar Bonavena was still a contender in 1968 and won solid decisions over Zora Folley, his first conqueror, and skillful Leotis Martin before getting a rematch in December against Joe Frazier. The fight was scheduled for a title-length fifteen rounds since it was for something called the New York State Athletic Commission championship. This time a more experienced Smokin' Joe, undefeated through twenty-one fights, attacked relentlessly, smothering Bonavena's power, and hammered him with left hooks to body and head. Bonavena responded with skill and determination – no more than two or three boxers at the time could have gone the distance with this Joe Frazier – but lost a lopsided unanimous decision.

There would be one more chance for glory: in December 1970 Muhammad Ali fought the second time since returning from exile, and Oscar Bonavena was his opponent. I watched the fight at my father's house in Bowling Green, Kentucky, worried that strong and unorthodox Bonavena was beating the world's most charismatic man. He never hurt Ali but hit him enough to make the fight close, and there was no indication Ali could stop Bonavena until a flash left hook in the fifteenth round knocked him down and Ali quickly floored him twice more to win by technical knockout. Ali proceeded to fight many of the most epic, and self-destructive, battles in ring history.

And Oscar Bonavena, who had fought four to eleven times a year during his career, faced only one opponent in each of the next two. At age twenty-nine, in early 1972, he appeared the last time in Madison Square and decked former two-time champion Floyd Patterson in the fourth round but lost a unanimous decision. In 1973 the man accustomed to fighting the best opponents faced only those with mediocre records. He began 1974 with a final attempt to regain stature, against Ron Lyle, who entered with but one loss and decisioned the aging Argentine.

Bonavena outpointed a good fighter, Larry Middleton, in his next fight but thereafter took on boxers who previously would have qualified only as his sparring partners. This kind of career slide is typical in boxing. And, indeed, a decline is inevitable in all sports. However, Oscar Bonavena's once-stimulating career ended with an avalanche of bad choices made by a deteriorating mind. After fighting only one time in 1975 and beating an unknown, Bonavena met Joe and Sally Conforte, owners of the infamous Mustang Ranch house of prostitution outside Reno. Joe hired Oscar to promote fights and train on his ranch that housed the family business.

Right away Bonavena, age thirty-three, began flirting and spending much private time with Sally, who was sixty years old and in poor health. Joe Conforte contended then and many years later that Bonavena did him a favor, taking his suddenly less-infirmed wife to town, and to bed, so Conforte could concentrate on young girlfriends. Sally was also busy funneling Mustang Ranch funds to fuel Bonavena's heavy gambling. She additionally served as his manager despite scant knowledge of boxing. Bonavena really didn't want to fight much anymore. He shaved sporadically, ignored his formerly-stylish locks that had evoked the nickname Ringo, gained weight, bore a marred and bloated face, and moved sluggishly during his final fight, a victory over another unknown in February 1976.

Three months earlier Mustang Ranch had burned down and local officials, many of whom Joe Conforte regularly bribed, declared it arson. That didn't derail Conforte, a prison veteran and unscrupulous entrepreneur. He built a much larger and nicer facility and secured it with two tall gun towers, an electric listening system inside and out, and banks of lights that automatically erupted at nightfall. There was a large and expensive grand opening party in early May 1976. Joe Conforte didn't attend. Sally played hostess. And Oscar Bonavena performed the role he'd been bragging about: he smoked cigars and grinned fatuously at guests he asked, "How do you like my joint?"

Two days later Joe Conforte ordered Oscar Bonavena and Sally to leave Mustang Ranch, and his several armed guards ensured compliance. One of them, Ross Brymer, also ransacked the boxer's trailer, removed his belongings, including his passport, and burned them. Conforte, and a henchman or two, later confronted Bonavena, handed him money for a return flight to Argentina, and told him to leave the country. Instead, the boxer drank and gambled the money away, and at six a.m. on May twenty-second drove up to the locked gate at Mustang Ranch, demanding to speak to Conforte. He wanted the harassment stopped and may still have deluded himself he could somehow acquire the life's work of a Sicilian immigrant. Conforte was supposedly asleep in the Blue Room, a special place at Mustang Ranch. His guards swore Bonavena was drunk and belligerent, and they repeatedly ordered him to leave. Only when Bonavena reached for a gun, they said, did Ross Brymer aim his powerful rifle, pull the trigger, and explode the heart of a man who had never taken the ten count. In a little while, as Conforte's employees stared at the body, he said, "What are you guys looking at? Haven't you ever seen a dead man?"

A pistol was found in Oscar Bonavena's boot. Was it planted? If not, was his addled mind and .07 percent blood alcohol level high enough to convince him he could take on a fortified guard corps framed by two gun towers. The only witnesses were the thugs working for Conforte. A jury, infested by six members who were tenants at various Conforte properties, convicted Ross Brymer not of murder but manslaughter. He was sentenced by a judge friendly to

Conforte, served fifteen months in prison, and died in 2000. Sally continued to manage Mustang Ranch behind the scenes until the IRS seized the property for back taxes in 1990. She died two years later from diabetes. Joe Conforte escaped to Brazil in 1991 before a grand jury could indict him for numerous financial crimes. In 1999 the Brazilian Supreme Court declined to expel Conforte, and he still lives there. Upon its return to Buenos Aires, the body of Oscar Bonavena lay in state at a sports arena. One hundred fifty thousand people walked by to say farewell to the toughest man in the history of Argentina.

Death in the Ring

When Is a Boxer Too Old?

This evening I pried through dusty file boxes to retrieve an article I wrote titled, "When Is a Boxer Too Old?" Now I'd answer everyone's born too old for a sport dedicated to brain busting. I'm not advocating a ban on boxing or mixed martial arts. That's unrealistic since the masses love violence, and I'm part of the illness since I used to spend plenty to see people fight in person and on pay per view. So I'm simply reviewing a sliver of the record: the once voluble Muhammad Ali hasn't spoken intelligibly in thirty years; the Quarry brothers, Jerry and Mike, proud contenders in the heavyweight and light heavy divisions, respectively, finished their lives as invalids and were buried in their fifties; Wilfred Benitez began his career as the slickest of defensive fighters, won his first world title at age seventeen and his third at twenty-two but soon slowed and became a slender target, and has been wheelchair bound and almost incoherent for years; Greg Page won a heavyweight title but fought too long and left his last fight paralyzed and died several years later; Duk-Koo Kim never opened his eyes after being battered on national television in 1982; more fighters than you can name barely speak today and will die much sooner than most contemporaries.

Let's assume that like ancient gladiators people will always fight professionally. Therefore, as I wrote in the 1980 story amplified here, it is unanimously acknowledged the aging process will eventually render all athletes incapable of competent performance. The uncertain issue has always been at what point the final disability occurs. Rudy Lester insisted his strength and durability still qualified him to be an amateur boxer despite being forty-three. Otis Grimble, who directed an amateur boxing tournament that week in Sacramento, thought Lester's athletic ability had declined to an unacceptable level and that's why he wouldn't let him enter the event. The state of Lester's health was a subjective matter that might never be agreed upon, even by physicians. But the boxer from Woodland claimed his constitutional right of due process was abrogated when Grimble denied his entry into the tournament: "I showed up for the weigh-in on Thursday morning, after filing my application on time, and Otis said, 'Hey, man, you're too old. You should be an official.'

"I told him I'd worked very hard and starved myself to get my weight down from one eight-five to one sixty-five and that this might be my last fight. Otis kept telling me how bad I looked getting knocked out. I asked him how it looked when young fighters got knocked out. It shouldn't matter what Otis thinks because I have a valid State Athletic Commission license and here it is. It wasn't fair for him to arbitrarily deny me the right to fight. Otis carries a vendetta because of a disagreement over renting a ring from the Police Athletic League (over which Grimble presides.)"

Grimble was presented Lester's arguments and responded, "I had to use my own judgment as tournament director. The welfare of all the participants is my responsibility. Rudy's too old. I've seen him fight and his legs get shaky every time he gets hit. Young guys could take those same punches without any problem. And I certainly don't have a vendetta against Rudy. He was a year late paying for the ring, but that was all right. We let Rudy ride back with us in our van from a boxing tournament in New Mexico. Is that a vendetta? The ring-renting incident happened in early 1978 and I allowed Rudy to fight in the 1978 and 1979 tournaments. He's been knocked out bad a few times."

At this point Bob Surkein, chairman of the National AAU, entered the discussion and said, "That's not Otis' decision. The tournament should have had a doctor state Lester was not qualified. If I'd been at the weigh-in, I'd have said you can't legally keep a guy out because of maximum age."

Then Grimble, himself a muscular man of forty-three, described another phase of the Rudy Lester case, "We held a Pacific AAU meeting in March and discussed Rudy for a half-hour. It was decided that he had to be examined by a doctor approved by the State Athletic Commission before he could fight again. Rudy didn't do that, so he couldn't fight."

"In that case, Otis acted properly," Surkein said. "Even though Lester has a valid licence until October 1980, his eligibility status can change from fight to fight. A fighter can be hurt bad enough in an instant to permanently disqualify himself from competition."

Rudy Lester still wanted to fight. He was proud of his 1978 tournament performance against a large heavyweight who twice decked him in the first round. Lester wobbled around the ring, holding onto his opponent and the ropes until the bell. Then, in the second, he landed a flashing right cross that knocked the young man unconscious. In the 1979 tournament, Lester led a light heavyweight in the third round when he caught a right that left him incoherent but on his feet. He was also stopped in a Carson City fight in February 1980.

"I can beat a lot of younger boxers. Almost everyone is knocked out once in a while," said Lester.

A generation later, I'm impressed by the vigor of this ancient boxing debate. The fighter's health is the essential issue, not whether he can win. Rudy Lester was right: he could, and did, beat many young opponents, but Otis Grimble was correct about a more important issue: Lester had already taken too much punishment and needed to be prohibited from fighting anymore. I wish professional boxers in the twenty-first century had to heed this irrefutable logic.

Incidentally, during the interview, Rudy Lester told me that he was seriously considering "kicking Otis' ass."

Since I'd seen Lester coldcock the heavyweight two years earlier, I worriedly conveyed his thoughts to Otis Grimble.

Extending muscular arms and squeezing my hands, he smiled and said, "What're you talking about? I'd whip Rudy's ass."

I'd still pay to see those two rumble, and that's the problem, isn't it?

Editorial note: At age fifty Otis Grimble placed a gun to his head. The newspaper article said only that he'd been having problems at home and work. He was a police officer and had recently done a public service television ad for the department. I was surprised how he'd grayed and by the sad expression of a man I'd considered gregarious. Grimble had boxed some as an amateur but probably not enough to sustain a serious brain injury. On the other hand...

Visiting Roberto Duran

Following his flight from Quito to Panama City, supposedly a quick stop en route to Houston, Fred asked a young lady working in an airport restaurant, "Does Roberto Duran still live here?"

"Oh, yes," she said. "He's got grandchildren as well as children, and they're on his reality TV show."

An eternal aficionado of boxing, Fred enlivened as he asked, "Where does Duran live?"

"I can't tell you that."

"I bet lots of people know."

"Why don't you go to his restaurant, La Tasca de Duran? They have lots of boxing photos on the walls and videos of his fights. You'll also probably see Roberto. He often comes in and talks to customers."

"Thanks," said Fred, who dashed to customer service, showed the lady in charge his tickets, and stated, "I've got to get my luggage now."

"That's impossible, sir," she said. "You'll have to sign these papers, and we'll send your luggage back here tomorrow from Houston."

"My luggage is already here."

"Yes, and it's en route to the plane you paid to have it sent to. Isn't your carry-on bag sufficient until tomorrow?"

Fred walked out the airport to hire a taxi for the trip to La Tasca de Duran. At dinnertime he entered a busy place, put his bag under the last table available, and ordered orange juice before he began to watch videos of Manos de Piedra – Hands of Stone – the greatest lightweight champion of the Twentieth Century and a devastating boxer at any weight. Fred remembered the first time he saw Roberto Duran fight. In June 1972 the dynamic and muscular young man, barely past his twenty-first birthday, challenged Ken Buchanan for the lightweight title in Madison Square Garden. As if he were in another street fight as a kid in the blighted El Chorrillo section of Panama City, Duran glowered at and cursed the champion, and then charged and pressured him, hooking, crossing, mauling, and ultimately flattening him in the thirteenth round with a shot to the testicles that, given the state of battle, was ignored and the referee raised the new champion's hand.

Roberto Duran soon demolished his next two opponents in the first round, making his record thirty-one and oh, and doubtless considered himself invincible in November 1972 when he moved up five pounds and returned to Madison Square Garden to fight Esteban De Jesus of Puerto Rico in a nontitle junior welterweight match. Facing an opponent of comparable strength for the first time, Duran was decked by a left hook. He got up quickly but could not overpower De Jesus and lost by unanimous decision.

He resumed campaigning as a lightweight and defeated ten foes, eight by knockout, over the ensuing sixteen months before defending his title against Esteban De Jesus in Panama City. This time Roberto Duran did not presume victory. He trained with conviction, summoned additional fury, and hammered the challenger until he wilted in the eleventh round.

Between fights Duran loved to eat and drink and dance and sing and hand out money to the poor people of Panama City. His frame bloated as his assets shriveled, and he generally struggled to lose dozens of pounds to make the lightweight limit of one hundred thirty-five. Thereafter, the issue wasn't winning or losing but whether Duran's opponent could go the distance. Only about one in four survived till the closing bell. In early 1978 he defended his lightweight title the final time, again stopping Esteban de Jesus, moving his record to sixty-three and one.

Before Duran's first major match at one hundred forty-seven pounds, in 1979, Fred had wondered if he could still be an overwhelming fighter against bigger men. His opponent, Carlos Palomino, until recently the welterweight champion, was an excellent puncher and boxer who'd lost his title on a disputed split decision against young Wilfred Benitez, at that juncture, early in his career, one of the best defensive fighters ever. Palomino believed he could overpower Roberto Duran. In fact, Duran proved stronger and quicker, and won every round. Palomino promptly retired and became an actor.

Duran next targeted Sugar Ray Leonard, the sleek young man who boxed and moved and, by so doing, enraged Duran who believed warriors stood and fought. He also craved Leonard's international popularity and the money the welterweight champion earned in and out of the ring. Prior to their fight in June 1980, at press conferences and public appearances, Duran cussed and threatened his nemesis. And he landed some psychic blows that intimidated Leonard, making him tentative early in the bout when Duran aggressively landed strong punches, staggered him once, and built a lead.

Fred sadly watched this sequence. Leonard, his favorite all-time fighter, after the great Ali, rallied before losing this time too. Okay, now show the rematch, Fred told a waiter. Be fair. Roberto Duran had returned on the Panamanian presidential jet to be received in the streets by the masses. They chanted his name and embraced him and together they rejoiced and partied. Duran gorged himself and gained ten, twenty, thirty, forty, fifty, sixty, seventy pounds as shrewd Leonard received reports and demanded a rematch soon as possible. The new welterweight champion should've said wait. Instead, five months later, after starving and dehydrating himself, he was facing a supremely trained and determined challenger who dodged his punches and mocked him, once rotating his right arm like a windmill before left jabbing a startled face, and would've delivered more physical and emotional punishment but Roberto Duran, the once-indomitable Hands of Stone, uttered the most infamous words in boxing history – "No mas" – and, despite being physically able to continue, walked away. Fred accepted his right to do so, but Duran had deprived the ticket-buying world of great drama.

No presidential plane waited to take Roberto Duran home this time. He returned to a country where men called him a coward, a queer, a fairy. Those men, one should note, invariably did so from the distance bigmouths prefer. Duran was humiliated and vowed, to generally skeptical listeners, that he'd regain his pride and reputation. He won two nondescript decisions in 1981 but then lost two decisions, one to Wilfred Benitez, the following year. Promoter and carnival barker Don King dropped him. So did most of his remaining fans. Duran pushed on into January 1983 against former welterweight champion Pipino Cuevas in Los Angeles. In what could be a final appearance center stage, he pressured the powerful left hooker who had weak defensive skills and stopped him in the fourth round, and afterward, alone with intimates, he proclaimed, "I've got it again."

Then he moved up to a hundred fifty-four pounds and battered undefeated Davey Moore, scoring a technical knockout, to win the junior middleweight title. Once more he was celebrated at home, and he thought, "These hypocrites are the same ones who degraded me." He would show them even more. He'd move up again and take on the most ferocious pound-for-pound fighter in the world, middleweight champion Marvin Hagler. Most boxers, gamblers, commentators, and fans said Hagler's going to pulverize Duran, and he's going to do so quickly. That's what Fred had thought and, looking at the start of their video, was still afraid for Duran. He ordered another orange juice. That calmed him. So did Duran's confidence and skill in the ring. He won several rounds before mean muscular Marvin Hagler roughed him up late and won a narrow unanimous decision.

This would've been a perfect exit for Roberto Duran, age thirty-two, a champion in three divisions and nearly a fourth, owner of a stellar seventy-seven and five record, a legend in the fistic world. Unfortunately, fighters rarely quit on time. They keep lurching into the ring. Duran next took on Thomas Hearns, the six-one Cobra who coiled before nailing his shorter opponent with right hands. The last one hit Duran on the forehead above his left eye and he fell face first onto the canvas, the only time he was ever incoherent in the ring. Surely, a man pole-axed like that the day before his thirty-third birthday, who'd been sparring regularly since age eight and a professional since sixteen, would say: enough.

That was in 1984 and Roberto Duran would fight thirty-seven more times over the ensuring seventeen years, winning twenty-six and losing ten in a career that touched five decades and spanned an astonishing thirty-three years and five months, until he was fifty. Much of the extended final phase Duran fought men who would have been unqualified to meet him in his prime. In 1987, at age thirty-seven, there'd been one more night of magic. Facing rugged Iran Barkley, the middleweight champion, Duran unleashed a combination of five punches, the last of which floored Barkley and enabled the Panamanian to win his fourth title. He then fought "Uno Mas" against an also-aging, though victorious, Sugar Ray Leonard, and many observers prayed, "No mas."

Maybe it'll be better if Roberto Duran doesn't come in tonight,

Fred thought. He's probably disfigured and punch drunk. Fred decided to eat somewhere else, finished his orange juice, and was putting his wallet in his left front pocket when in he walked, Manos de Piedra, still striding like a champion, moving around his restaurant, shaking hands, patting shoulders, smiling, posing for pictures, usually speaking Spanish, tossing in some English, laughing, the star of the show. Fred stood and said, "Mucho gusto."

"Oh, you speak Spanish," said Roberto Duran. "I'm going to sing in a little while. Stay for the show."

"Absolutely," said Fred.

The George Foreman Addiction

If you watch George Foreman fight, admit it. You're not seeking ballet. You yearn to see men clubbed in the head and knocked senseless or out, and you're probably not to blame. Your addiction to Foreman happens unexpectedly, during the sixty-eight Olympics. TV schedules aren't as precise in those days, and you think you'll be watching Tommie Smith and John Carlos and Jimmy Hines sprint through thin Mexico City air. You want to see Bob Beamon soar in the long jump. You're excited about Kip Keino and Jim Ryun dueling over fifteen hundred meters. You only find George Foreman by accident. You haven't imagined a nineteen-year-old Hercules who batters opponents with jabs like a felled tree swinging horizontally from a chain, and insist you don't entirely enjoy seeing Russian miner Ionas Chapulos catching those jabs, bleeding in the first round, and getting hammered by combinations in the second. You're watching for patriotic reasons. While Smith and Carlos extend black gloves of protest on the medal stand, and thousands of fresh young Mexican corpses rot in graves of dissent, George Foreman displays the American flag and bows in four directions.

In honor of his patriotism you resolve to support George as a pro. Discharging thunder with each hand he knocks out his first seven opponents before winning by decision. After three more destructions you forgive him when another foe survives the distance, and you're likewise understanding when he only stops three more before having to go ten rounds against Gregorio Peralta and even losing some of those en route to a unanimous decision. George Foreman agrees with you. Something ain't right if the opponent's still standing at the final bell. Eating and exercising more, and swinging wider and harder, the surly young man bombards most foes early and knocks out a stunning twenty-four straight. Even granite-head George Chuvalo is helpless by the third, and Foreman yells at the referee to stop the fight or he'll kill Chuvalo, the same man who before and after this goes the distance with Muhammad Ali.

Most astonishing is George's fight against Joe Frazier for the world heavyweight title in January seventy-three. Smokin' Joe's also undefeated and has pulverized most opponents. And he's the favorite. Experts say he's going to be too quick for Foreman. You fear they're correct. Instead, in the first round big George manhandles the champion and lands a powerful overhand right to his head that causes a friend, sitting next to you in the pay-per-view theater, to jump up. A rough voice behind says sit down. What a foolish sentiment. Soon everyone's standing and roaring as Foreman floors Frazier three times and thrice more in the second, sometimes launching the champ into the air and once knocking him down as, in a stupor, he turns and tries to dash away.

Two fights later you're worried. Ken Norton, breaker of Ali's jaw and twice his conqueror, though only once officially, is going after George's crown. As fighters receive final instructions you're relieved that sculpted Norton looks rather slender next to big George who lands a right hand under the heart and pursues a retreating challenger in the first round. Muhammad Ali provides ringside commentary and optimistic belief that his nemesis Norton is fighting well and says he's proud of him. A couple of minutes later George's pounding Norton with right hands an elephant might throw and Norton falls into the ropes and receives an eight count and soon catches a thudding left that knocks him against the ropes and then eats a right uppercut and goes down to end this fight.

You feel sorry for Muhammad Ali. The only two men who've beaten him up are inadequate against ill-tempered George Foreman. Why doesn't Ali simply retire? He'll never regain the title. Foreman will kill him in Africa in seventy-four. Even after being cut and unable to spar for a month while he trains for the postponed fight, Foreman's favored by smart guys like you. He'll nail Ali with some of those slow wide punches he's launching. Ali shouldn't be on the ropes. You and the fans in the big-screened auditorium think he's making it easier for the champion. But Joe Frazier's tells people near ringside he doesn't think heavy-breathing Foreman is going to make it. Joe's jealous. You know George'll soon settle this. When Ali erupts from the ropes and fires a right dropping the champion, you're sure he'll get up and, at the count of ten, he does.

George Foreman doesn't fight in seventy-five. He comes back angry early in seventy-six against ex-con Ron Lyle who almost flattens him with a right cross in the first round. George staggers and holds and survives. In the second he hurts Lyle. In the fourth, however, Lyle knocks George down and moves in for destruction. But George then floors Lyle and prepares to finish him. Lyle responds by decking George. You're growling on the living room floor. You don't growl during football and basketball games. Why now? You're not the only animal. This slugfest is voted fight of the year, and in the fifth round poor Lyle catches many undefended headshots and collapses.

A few months later George again overwhelms Joe Frazier and stops three other guys before facing slick Jimmy Young in seventy-seven. Young's a smaller, lighter-hitting version of Ali. He can't win by knock out. But George can. There it is, a huge left in the seventh round, and Young's ready to go. He's hiding but George is after him and will get him. He almost does but Young survives and plays mister graceful and wears him out and even puts him down briefly late in the twelfth before exhausted George arises and chases a ghost. In the loser's dressing room he's sucked into hell before God rescues him and demands he quit fighting and start preaching. George Foreman complies, and you say farewell to the greatest slugger ever.

You're distressed but know you'll survive. Ken Norton and Larry Holmes pound each other for fifteen rounds in seventy-eight. And Ali again reclines against the ropes, this time for fifteen rounds against smaller Leon Spinks, who should've been his sparring partner but now's world champ. There are young slugger's aplenty. Marvin Hagler and Sugar Ray Leonard and Tommy Hearns and Roberto Duran are in their prime and hammering people. But these biggest stars are little guys. You want some heavyweight power and in the mid-eighties are thankful Iron Mike Tyson appears and destroys everyone in the ring and some outside.

And in eighty-seven, ten years after his last fight, George Foreman says he's coming back. He needs money for his ministry. That's no doubt true but you know he misses hitting people in the head. Fans of demolition don't think Foreman can hurt people anymore and are quite insulting about his antiquity, age thirty-eight, and his girth, two hundred sixty-seven flabby pounds. Though less stylish than earlier, George resumes battering foes and, while losing weight, ignores those who cry the competition isn't much. Bull-feathers, you say: a knockout's a knockout. And what's insignificant about stopping former light heavyweight and cruiserweight champion

Dwight Muhammad Qawi in seven.

Like you, many fans start getting that old excitement while George poleaxes his first eighteen comeback opponents. Now he's back on page one and national TV and the advertisers want to ride the fists of a man who's replaced his scowl and hard words with a smile and charming stories. Hard-hooking but long-inactive Gerry Cooney is bombed out in the second round, and his respected trainer Gil Clancy, interviewed afterward in the ring, says damn right George Foreman can win the heavyweight title, he throws bombs and they land. Delightful destruction continues with five more wins in ninety, and in April the following year George boasts twenty-four straight victories, all but one by knockout, when he battles champion Evander Holyfield. To see this one you've got to unload big pay-per-view bucks, and you eagerly do so but cringe while young, quick Holyfield gives ponderous George a frightful thrashing and wins a unanimous decision to defend his title.

Two years later, in ninety-three, Tommy Morrison outboxes immobile George Foreman, age forty-four, and you wish you could talk to the former champ and tell him to give it up. He's proved his thesis. Vigorous life continues in the forties. Quit now and don't end up permanently injured like Ali. George may have been ready to do so but divine assistance arrives: without fighting for seventeen months, the aged slugger is awarded a shot at the heavyweight title of undefeated Michael Moorer. You're again happy to pay to watch but often wince as Moorer lashes Foreman much like Holyfield had three years earlier. It's sad seeing a special champion get whipped. And the predictability becomes boring. You resolve not to watch George fight any more, after tonight. You even consider turning off the damn TV. Are you reaching for the button when George lands a strong right cross and two seconds later follows with another pile-driving right that knocks Moorer onto the canvas and out? You wouldn't have touched the dial. You're jumping and rejoicing. A man of forty-five has just become heavyweight champion of the world.

George is hot now and engulfed by fans, talk show hosts, journalists, and advertisers. A shrewd group has developed a grill that supposedly drains much of the fat from meat while cooking it and signs the new champ to promote what becomes the George

Death in the Ring

Foreman Grill. The big happy raconteur convinces folks this is for their health. For his, George fights only four times the next three years. He never stops anyone after Michael Moorer. It doesn't matter. You and a hundred million others buy his grill and are delighted when the corporation pays him about two hundred millions dollars in commissions and buyout fees. That's George Foreman's greatest knockout.

George Thomas Clark

Toe to Toe with Bobby Chacon

You've got to be ready in the San Fernando Valley. People will test you, especially when you're a little guy. At school and especially on the streets lots of punks come after me, and I kick the shit out of most. They can't believe my punches. And, really, I'm surprised, too. I get so I enjoy being challenged. Why not? I'm not big enough for football or baseball.

My girlfriend Valerie and I love watching pros fight on TV. You can beat them, Bobby, she says. Those are big guys, I tell her. No, she says, look at their weight, about like yours. I figure I'll try. I start working out in a guy's garage and in local gyms and get my ass kicked at first. I lose twenty pounds and learn I'm a quick featherweight. My trainer Joe Ponce teaches me to move my head and dodge punches. And I've still got the power I had on the streets, knocking out a few amateurs. I know I'm ready to go pro but Joe makes me wait till I'm twenty. By then Val and I are married.

I debut in 1972 and stop seventeen of my first nineteen opponents and am ready for Ruben Olivares, former bantamweight champion, who I already beat pretty good when I was his sparring partner. He doesn't like training. He's a partier. So am I, but I'm naturally bigger. I won't make excuses. Olivares has more than seventy fights and he takes me to school, stops me in the ninth round.

I don't worry too much. I start knocking people out again. In May 1974 I take on undefeated Danny Lopez. All of L.A. and fans around the country and the world are watching us. And they're thrilled. It's a war. Someone hits me, no matter how hard, I don't back off, not much, not for long. I counterattack. I know I can take more than anyone. And I hit harder. Danny Lopez is a helluva fighter. The fans want blood, doesn't matter whose. Finally, I knock Lopez down in the ninth and the referee stops the fight. Now I'm getting big-time coverage in L.A.

Everyone's more excited that September when I stop Alfredo Marcano to win the world featherweight title. I'm the best in the world, man. I get so many invitations from incredible women who tell me I'm handsome and cool. I don't go around saying that. I don't have to. I still love Val but I've got to live like a champ. I drink quite a bit and sometimes do some other stuff too. I can work it off. Ask Jesus Estrada, the guy I knock out in round two of my first title defense. Now I'm going to get revenge against Ruben Olivares.

Maybe I should be training harder in 1975. Some people tell me I'm getting a little fat. My inner circle, which keeps getting bigger and more loyal, tells critics to fuck off, Bobby's the man. I'll be all right. But, ten days before the fight, I shouldn't be sixteen pounds overweight. I have to starve and sweat weight off and Olivares laughs at me at the weigh-in. Knowing I'm weak, he attacks and knocks me down twice in the second round and that's it.

A few months later I lose a unanimous decision to Bazooka Limon and in 1976 a guy with a losing record decks me twice and busts me up. Val rushes into the dressing room and tells me and the press I should retire. I agree. I'm the one getting hit. I need some free time. Sure, plenty of women are around, and my buddies and I do some drinking and snorting. Everybody's doing it. Okay, Val gets upset and leaves. She's a beautiful girl and I love her but she's home all the time and not doing anything but raising three kids and sometimes she bores me.

She comes back to me, and I return to the ring and pound people. In 1977 I finally get another rematch with Ruben Olivares. This time I'm too strong and win a unanimous decision. I've earned another title shot but they jack me around till 1979 and match me with Alexis Arguello for the super featherweight title. I duck under his long arms and am beating him for five rounds but he busts my eye open in the sixth and next round his left hook rattles my head and makes me squat for an eight count and soon the fight's over.

Val insists I quit. I say yes. I say maybe. I say we'll see. She thinks moving onto twenty acres near Oroville north of Sacramento will solve everything. Okay, let's try. I'm a long way from L.A. but it's still my brain and I want another shot at the super featherweight crown, this time against Cornelius Boza-Edwards in 1981. He's a big dude for a hundred thirty pounds, believe me, but I'm not scared. I go after him. He's not scared either and beats hell out of me. I'm through after thirteen rounds.

When I get home Val's on me again to quit. Sometimes I say I will but really know I won't. I love to fight. It's all I've ever done.

Val needs to understand that instead of getting paranoid and depressed and arguing with me all the time and taking pills. I'm a fighter, okay. In February 1982 I'm in Sacramento for a bout and Val locks the bedroom door and tries to overdose. Her brother comes over and removes the door and gets her to the hospital on time. Val wakes up mad as hell to be alive and pulls tubes out of her arms and storms out of the hospital and runs away. We can't find her for a month. Then they see her at the Sacramento airport. She's confused, talking about guns.

I drive down and get her. She's lost weight but still looks great. On the way home she knows I'm already preparing for another fight, in March. I tell her, yeah, I'm going to quit but I gotta win another title first. Day before fight I get the devastating call: Val's shot herself. She's gone. I race home and hold her. There's nothing more I can do. I guess I never could do anything, even call a psychiatrist. I have a life outside the house. It's passion that pulls me back to Sacramento the next day to knock out Salvador Ugalde. Right away I beat two more guys. I gotta keep busy, keep living.

I find a new girlfriend, soon my wife, and in December 1982 get that title shot, against my old rival Bazooka Limon. In our three fights we each have a win and a draw. In this fourth bout I know my fans in Sacramento are worried when Bazooka forces me onto the ropes and pounds me. They're figuring what many have said, he's got great stamina and wears opponents down and he's younger than Bobby, too. I answer with right hands to Bazooka's face, backing him up. I wobble him in the ninth. His left cross decks me in the tenth and he punishes me in the eleventh. We simultaneously stagger each other in the thirteenth but he's the one on rubbery legs. I have a new level of endurance and stun him in the fourteenth, so it's meaningless when he raises his arms in victory. I'm the aggressor in the fifteenth, and late in the round I chase him and land a right and then another puts him on his back. He gets up but that knockdown gives me two points I need to win by close unanimous decision. Old Memorial Auditorium is a riot. So are living rooms around the country. People have seen a war, the fight of the year.

In May 1983 I have another fight of the year. That's an honor but also means the boxers have kicked the crap out of each other. I floor Cornelius Boza-Edwards in the first and second rounds. He decks me in the third. He pounds me on the ropes. He cuts my eye. I look like I can't survive. In the seventh the ring doctor threatens to stop the fight. He can't stop it long as I fight and keep hitting Boza-Edwards with right hands. He's getting tired. I can feel it. I see it. In the twelfth I flatten him again. He's up but no longer dangerous. The title's still mine.

And I want another one, the lightweight title of Ray Mancini. Everyone says Ray's too big and strong. And you know what? They're right. He beats me up and they stop it in the third round. I'm pretty frustrated but that's no excuse. Neither are booze and meth. Maybe my second wife had something to do with it. Anyway, I slap her around pretty good. But I don't use my fists. Never would. The judge gives me probation.

I keep fighting and getting hit but hit back harder. In 1987 I go to jail a few months for a violating probation. An unknown guy also knocks me down three times before I stop him. People say quit, Bobby, you're slurring your words. I am not, not much. And I don't care. I don't want to quit. I'd rather fight a guy who's lost twice as many as he's won. Okay, I'm done.

I've got other commitments, kids to raise, more women to marry, lots more drugs to take. I disappear into Arizona for about a month. Everyone's worried. Not me. When they find me they ask what have you been doing, Bobby? I laugh and say who the hell knows.

I do know most of my friends have disappeared. I guess they liked the money more than me. Maybe they're ashamed to hang out with a guy who lives in a flophouse and collects cans to recycle. It's good work. I also train kids to box when I can. And my own kids are big now, the two who survived. My son was murdered a long time ago. I still miss him and Valerie, the best of four wives. When I was boxing I thought I was over her, but now I'm not. I'm thankful to be at the wedding of my daughter. Watch the video of me dancing. I still got rhythm. That's what I know. Know what I forget? I forgot.

George Thomas Clark

Pursuing Pipino Cuevas

Almost a century ago legendary sportswriters crafted vibrant stories about what they'd seen and imagined, and later regaled each other while consuming vast quantities of spirits. In the late 1970s, when I was a newspaper correspondent, the dynamics had shifted and reporters often wrote tepid articles, the stuff of wire-service drones, and sometimes imbibed beforehand. One such fellow where I worked had been bestowed the entire world of boxing, and no one else was allowed a word on the subject. Like a serf I accepted this fatuity, and was thus standing unarmed, without paper or pen, at aging Capital Boxing Gym when world welterweight champion Pipino Cuevas held his first workout in Sacramento, where he would fight local brawler Pete Ranzany.

Reporters from the smaller local newspaper were there, the television stations were fully represented, and several radio stations sent people. Only the proud paper of record had failed to cover this event, significant since it presaged the city's first world championship fight. Despite having hungrily and unsuccessfully pursed opportunities to write about boxing, I really did not want to work this day. I stood chatting with fans, enjoying the energy, until seized by responsibility. My newspaper, which wasn't really mine since I was a mere stringer, needed me. From a generous scribe I borrowed the necessary equipment, took notes, and, with help from a Spanish translator I wouldn't need today, interviewed Cuevas' trainer, Lupe Sanchez. I then sped to the newsroom, found a vacant video display terminal – they still weren't called computers – and wrote a story I eagerly presented to the bureaucrat who'd somehow become editor. Instead of saying, "Nice work filling the void caused by my incompetence," he grimaced and groaned that ole moonshine was covering all aspects of the fight and that I had to confine myself to high school sports.

What could I do in this hellish, pre-website world? I called the sports editor of the Woodland newspaper, told him what I had, and he said, "Bring it up. I'll give you a dollar."

"Can't you go five?"

"Only one."

I drove about forty miles roundtrip to Woodland, burning a lot more than a buck of gas, and gave my story to a man too genial and open-minded for editorship at a big-city newspaper. He read the story and said, "I like it," and handed me the most delightful dollar I'll ever earn.

Here, slightly altered, is what I wrote:

Lupe Sanchez, Cuevas' manager, entered Capital Boxing Gym first, scanned the room, and stepped aside as the champion walked in out of the rain and wiped his feet on a mat. Staring straight ahead, Cuevas moved directly to the dressing room, followed by stablemates Jose Palacios, Marcos Geraldo, Moises Sore, Julio Mendez, and Sal Lopez of Sacramento, who will debut on the undercard. While the boxers were dressing, Sanchez checked to ensure all equipment was satisfactory and that spectators and media wouldn't disturb his fighters. In about 15 minutes each man was introduced as he came out to have his hands taped.

Cuevas and Sore were the first to spar, and the champion immediately showed he's an aggressive trainer, boring in and raking Sore's body and head with long left and right hooks. Cuevas also peppered him with crisp left jabs that thudded against headgear and snapped Sore's head back. Lupe Sanchez, standing in a corner of the ring, several times told the fighters to take it easy, saying, "Despacio, despacio."

Though not as muscular as Cuevas, Sore was able to hit him regularly. Cuevas has a pulverizing left hook that enabled him to win the title at age eighteen, but he holds his hands low, concentrating on offense and exposing his chin and kidneys. These alluring targets aren't hit much since Cuevas has stopped seven straight opponents while winning and defending the title. During his sparring session with Mendez, only a lightweight, Cuevas reduced the power of his punches a little and periodically tapped his headgear, signaling to punch him a few times.

After sparring four rounds, Cuevas worked three rounds on the speed bag, backhanding it with both fists and then letting it swing slowly before clobbering it with roundhouse rights and lefts. Sanchez scrutinized Cuevas throughout the training session and gave instructions in a soft voice. The old man kept track of time on his wristwatch, saying "medio" for half a minute left and "diez" for ten seconds. He turned the next training duty over to an assistant who put on gloves that looked like catchers mitts and thrust them from side to side, providing moving targets for Cuevas' explosive punches. He finished his regimen with rope jumping, shadow boxing, and sit-ups done on a short table. His legs were held at a point that placed his rear on the edge of the table, enabling him to bend back and lower his head to the floor before curling up and touching his forehead to his knees.

When Cuevas returned to the dressing room, I approached Sanchez and, through a translator, requested a few minutes. He nodded.

"Pete Ranzany is probably the best puncher that Pipino has fought and might be able to shake him up," I said.

"Ranzany thinks he's the hardest puncher Pipino's ever fought, but he's not," said Sanchez. "Angel Espada hits harder. So does Harold Weston. Pipino is much stronger than Ranzany."

Perhaps Espada is in the same punching league with Ranzany, but Weston definitely is not. And Sanchez probably realizes this. But he, like the entire Cuevas camp, is confident the champ can overpower any welterweight in the world.

"I think Ranzany's a little quicker than Pipino," I said. "His punches are short and straight whereas Pipino's are delivered in long, hooking motions."

"No, no," said Sanchez. "Pipino is quicker."

"Ranzany's five-ten and a half and Pipino is only five-eight and a half. Ranzany will have a reach advantage," I said.

Lupe Sanchez smiled at me and winked. "Pipino knows how to take advantage of a disadvantage."

Writing today, I can report that Lupe Sanchez understood this matchup far better than I. Fighting before a large outdoor crowd in Hughes Stadium, Pete Ranzany aroused his fans by occasionally hitting Cuevas in the first round and avoiding most of the champion's roundhouse lefts and rights. In the second Cuevas landed many power punches, decked the challenger twice, and punished him until the referee stopped the fight. As disconsolate Ranzany walked through drizzle toward the dressing room, a man nearby said, "Don't worry, Pete, Sacramento still loves you."

Puerto Rican Trilogy

Edwin Rosario at Home

I grow up poor and start fighting for money at age fifteen and win my first world title at twenty and earn millions and my fourth title at twenty-eight. I deserve some fun and take advantage that women and fans love me and impressive guys are friends who give me drugs. Then I have to buy them. That's okay. I'm living wild and need a fix or booze but can't afford either so take a case of beer and get arrested and have other problems leading to a year in prison. When I get out I've lost homes and cars and my wife but still have four daughters. And I know I've still got knockout power. Maybe I'm an old thirty-four but don't dwell on that. I'm proud I went through rehab. I'm ready to win another title, and soon beat five guys who aren't very good. I'm not worried about them now. I'm visiting my daughters but don't feel well and have to go home. Now I'm living with my parents who know I'm not right. Less than an hour later Dad checks and I'm gone.

The Hector Camacho Experience

I'm only fifteen but in jail and then out I can't slow down and don't want to everything's moving so fast I have to fight fuck dance and talk and I love speeding in stolen cars and taking other things and get more excited in the ring. I'm so much quicker than opponents I belt whenever I want while dodging their punches and prancing away. I'm a father at sixteen when I start winning amateur titles and pound Bazooka Limon for the world junior lightweight championship at twenty-one. It's really incredible all the girls tell me I'm so handsome and cool which I know I am so wired I can't stop doing things to make me feel better that's what coke does I do so much and tell friends and reporters I know I'm going out by bullets I think about that all the time. How are you going to die? I can't wait I win the lightweight title at twenty-three I'm making millions I'm the macho man of boxing and keep winning at twenty-eight I'm thirty-eight and oh no one can beat me as I enter the ring in Roman armor or Indian headdress or fox fur robe. I'm way too tough for cops and guys in nightclubs I'm the macho man they rob giving Greg Haugen a split decision I get the title back three months later and at twenty-nine I'm in the showdown of Latin idols against plodding Julio Cesar Chavez. He can't catch me he can't keep catching me he can't keep doing this he's beating hell out of me they say I'm a runner I'm a dancer I don't like to get hit. You like getting hit? I'm getting hit by everything Chavez has but don't go down and keep fighting a lion who wins about every round but I raise my hands.

I'm a warrior and still the pretty macho man and at thirty-one move up to welterweight and go after Felix Trinidad's crown in a war for Puerto Rican rights they're mine though I'm more from New York it doesn't matter this guy's eleven years younger and too big but can't stop me. I keep fighting and winning and batter old legends Roberto Duran and Sugar Ray Leonard I love those guys they help me get ready at thirty-five to take on another Latin heartthrob Oscar de la Hoya who's too young and slick and knocks me down but I get up no one's stopping the macho man. I don't lose for six years when I'm almost forty-one I'm not afraid and keep beating guys outside the ring and ladies still love me but they and my four sons and ex wife are expensive and coke's worse and why I love it so much people don't understand. Here try it and you'll see how great it is. I'm almost forty-three and four times a world champion breaking into an electronics store for a payday that ends with my hands in cuffs and ecstasy confiscated but my lawyers keep me out of prison so I can hang out and snort more coke and get shot at in twenty-eleven and a month later I pick up one of my sons by the neck and slam before stomping him. We'll fix that in court. What the hell I've got places in Florida and Puerto Rico and at fifty I'm loving life on the island and my buddy and I have ten packets of coke in his car and snort one and are ready to do lots more when I'm shot in the face by a guy you know's too scared to step up and take on the macho man of boxing.

Death in the Ring

Try Hitting Wilfred Benitez

You can't hit me. I see punches coming before they're thrown and move my head left right back up and down all over again making you hit air where I should've been. I'm so mature, turning pro when I'm fifteen and in little more than two years confusing a great champion, Antonio Cervantes, to win the junior welterweight title, youngest ever to do so. Looks like I'll be champion forever. I keep moving and confusing everyone so can't believe Bruce Curry knocks me down when I'm nineteen. I get up and go right back down and also fall once in the fifth but win a split decision and handle him my next fight. I can't make a hundred forty anymore, I'm only nineteen and growing into a welterweight and in a year win that title, beating a fine champion, Carlos Palomino. Now I'm twenty-one and ready for the biggest fight in the world, defending my title against another unbeaten, Sugar Ray Leonard. I'm still slick but on this night Leonard's smoother and stronger and stops me in the fifteenth round. Okay, I tell the world in English, we fight, he win. No problem. I win three fights in a row, getting heavier and stronger, and pound Maurice Hope to capture my third world title. I'm only twenty-two. I'll be king forever, especially after I teach defense to Roberto Duran, who barely hits me. I'm rich and sexy and a hero in Puerto Rico and everywhere else I go.

Next fight I stick my nose under Tommy Hearns' chin during the pre-fight stare down. I look calm but understand he's one big dude and, despite dodging dozens of his blows, absorb enough to lose the decision and feel bad a long time. I'll be all right. I'm only twenty-four and master of defense. I'll show rough left-handed Syrian middleweight Mustafa Hamsho. I'll dodge and dance and pop. Maybe I will next time. Tonight Hamsho kicks ass, and next year Davey Moore stops me in the second round. Hold it. Sugar Ray Leonard needed fifteen rounds to get me, and Hearns couldn't stop me in fifteen nor Hamsho in twelve. What's going on? Some tell me I still have only the strength of a junior welterweight but am slower and shouldn't fights guys like Mathew Hilton, a burly Canadian who mauls me nine rounds before backing me onto the ropes and knocking me out with a roundhouse that blasts my head back and jars my mouth eerily open. I watch replays on film. I can't stand to watch. I'm only twenty-seven. What the hell's happening? Maybe I'm an old twenty-seven. I conclude I'm an old twenty-eight when a journeyman beats me up in Argentina and I lose my documents and stumble around that country for a year or two. I'm retired. That's a good move. Three and a half years later I'm back for four fights, two losses, and lots more shots to the head. But I don't think those last four fights are the problem. It's the punches I took as a kid, and the punches I absorbed as a pro, and the way my brain keeps getting worse, often making me forget who I am. Thankfully, I have a small pension, a sturdy wheelchair, and plenty of relatives to care for me.

Temperament Wins

On a June 1991 Sacramento night at Arco Arena, hometown junior welterweight champion Loreto Garza defended his title against Edwin Rosario, who despite being only twenty-eight and a three-time lightweight titlist was perceived to be in decline and a dramatic underdog. Perhaps oddsmakers believed Rosario had already crumbled from abuse of alcohol and other drugs.

It's unlikely Loreto Garza viewed Edwin Rosario as a diminished opponent, and certain Rosario decked him with a right hook seconds into the fight. Garza could've been excused for staying down, but he got up and was floored again. He arose on wobbly legs and, despite more punishment, survived until the bell. In the third round another Rosario right rocked Garza and a flurry knocked him down. Soon he was down again and a former champion.

The outcome of this fight was largely irrelevant to the life of each man. Loreto Garza didn't need boxing or the title he'd won a year earlier by dominating Vinny Pazienza. He had something more important: personal stability. I was impressed he'd said in a newspaper interview that he never used boxing skills to settle disputes because "it took a lot" to provoke him. His feelings about meeting the woman who became his wife also resonated. He simply said he'd immediately felt good and natural being with her. People don't need Garza's left jab and right cross, they need his central nervous system.

After losing to Edwin Rosario, Loreto Garza knocked out three undistinguished opponents and retired at age thirty. He had a family and wanted to preserve his health. He also had a new career with the California Youth Authority. Several years later he transferred to the transportation team at the California Medical Facility. In a 2013 trade newsletter, Garza's colleagues made predictable comments:

"You represent the department…with incredible humility. I have always respected you even though it took this many years to find out you are a great champion."

"You are not just a good boxer but you are a great person. Everyone who knows you must be lucky."

"I had the privilege of working with Loreto…His humbleness and sense of humor are a breath of fresh air in this, at times, tension-filled job."

In his next fight Edwin Rosario lost the new title by technical knockout and was stopped again two fights later. He then abandoned boxing four years during which he nearly drank and drugged himself to death and did destroy his family life, squander his fortune, and rot a year in prison. In 1997 he began a comeback, defeating several opponents who had no chance. On a December evening that year he visited his four daughters but felt ill and returned to the house of his parents, where he resided. Less than an hour later he was dead, not because he was a bad person but because he lacked stability, the essential gift.

Memories of Emanuel Steward

The email from a friend dropped in my box and simply said: "RIP Emanuel Steward." I thought this is a mistake, it must be, Steward always looks healthy on TV, and he's a winner who'll live a long time, it must be another guy with the same name who, quickly and privately, withered at age sixty-eight and died from diverticulosis. I checked it out and learned, no, it was the man who'd sculpted boxers as Michelangelo did marble, the artist who took kids from Detroit ghettos of barred windows and torched buildings and, in the sweltering basement of legendary Kronk Gym, taught them to become champions. He was the foremost boxing trainer of his generation and more, the man whose list of titlists is too long to quote but features Thomas Hearns, the Motor City Cobra, who became the first fighter to capture five world championships, and Milton McCrory, and Mike McCallum, and Gerald McClellan, and Michael Moorer, who won light heavyweight and heavyweight crowns, and it includes European heavyweights Lennox Lewis and Wladimir Klitschko, both already accomplished but in need of better technique they acquired from Steward prior to dominating their division. He also prepared Oscar de la Hoya and Evander Holyfield for some major fights and worked with thousands of obscure youngsters. Most he touched became better boxers. Steward himself had been a good amateur, a national Golden Gloves champ, but quit fighting and, to support wife and child, shivered on Detroit Edison utility poles before he committed to a career at ringside.

Whether training fighters, negotiating their contracts, serving as a boxing commentator on TV, or talking to journalists, Emanuel Steward was a man people enjoyed listening to. I know. I met him in 1980 when he visited Sacramento. In my capacity as a correspondent I called him at his motel and heard a man emerge from sleep as he said he couldn't see me then but to come by in an hour. Accompanied by the man who sent the email above, and another friend, I at the appointed time walked to the room of the trainer, who was then only thirty-six. This is an enhanced version of what I wrote:

After letting us in Emanuel Steward returned to bed, stretched onto his back, and spoke hoarsely until he fully awakened. Lounging isn't his normal daytime activity. He's often training welterweight champion Tommy Hearns and other boxers at Kronk Gym in a poor Polish and black neighborhood in Detroit. Many little boys identify more with the city's best fighters than their parents or teachers, and dream of winning fortunes as professionals. Steward, as Detroit's director of boxing, often begins molding students young as age seven. Their sacrifices and his guidance have generated two world champions – lightweight Hilmer Kenty being the other – and his top six fighters have a combined record of ninety-two and one with seventy-five knockouts. Now Steward's a roving professor of pugilism. Last night he was in Miami to help his newest protégé, Davey Armstrong, gain his sixth consecutive victory. Then he caught the red-eye flight to San Francisco, where he had a four-hour layover before coming here to hold a clinic for the Golden Bear Boxing Tournament.

"I do a lot of traveling," he said. "I've spent $42,000 on airfare so far this year. Where does that come from? From my own finances. I'm going to make about a million dollars this year.

"We take these small kids and tutor them for years. They're watched closely and brought along carefully. They get good competition and that breeds improvement. Those tough cities in the East like Chicago, Detroit, New York and Philadelphia make tough fighters. The economic conditions make a guy hungrier. There's a very high activity and competition level in the East, much higher than in the West.

"Most of my kids have had a good apprenticeship, starting at an early age in our amateur program. If a kid hasn't had extensive experience as an amateur, I don't want to be bothered with him. We run a rough ass gym. Some top pros come to work out with us, but they leave because they can't take it. Babs McCarthy, your guy from Sacramento, was an exception to that. Babs isn't all that skillful, but he's tough and not too many top fighters can beat him." (A few years later McCarthy drowned, or was dumped into a river, and no one claimed his body for several days.)

Hearns, the stable's most publicized member, galvanized boxing fans in July with a precise and brutal second-round knockout of Pipino Cuevas in their title fight. Hearns appeared a towering light heavyweight bullying an overmatched welterweight.

"Tommy is officially six-foot-one but he's almost six-three, about the same height as Muhammad Ali," said Steward. "Tommy's potential is unlimited. His strength is unbelievable. He sparred with light heavyweight champion Matthew Saad Muhammad and was strong enough for Matthew. In training Tommy usually works with light heavies because he's just too strong for welterweights. But Tommy has his hands full in the gym. Then, in fights, he destroys guys.

"Despite what people say, Tommy doesn't have any trouble making the 147-pound limit. Eventually, I expect he'll become a middleweight and win the title. I think he can beat any middleweight right now. He could eventually become light heavyweight champ." (Hearns would indeed take that title in 1991, decisioning Virgil Hill.)

When the future of Tommy Hearns is discussed, the name Sugar Ray Leonard usually follows. Hearns was too young and slender to compete for the 1976 national boxing team, and toiled in the basement of Kronk Gym as Leonard smiled luminously on television screens around the world and dominated opponents to win the gold medal at the Summer Olympics in Montreal. From his professional debut several months later, Leonard earned large purses in numerous nationally-televised fights. He's effervescent and charming while Hearns is shy and inarticulate. Leonard plays Ali to Hearn's Joe Frazier. A collision is inevitable.

"Styles make fights and Leonard's style could cause Tommy some trouble," the trainer said. "But if Leonard gets hurt in the second round, like he did against Roberto Duran, he won't make it. Tommy will knock him out."

In fact, Emanuel Steward said Hearns had already stopped Leonard – twice. In 1980 Steward insisted that I not attribute this information to him – he didn't want to show disrespect for Leonard – but now let's put it in quotes. "In two 1978 workouts in Baltimore, held two days apart, Tommy pounded Leonard until he was unable to continue. He was helpless against the ropes."

The first time they fought publicly, in 1981, Hearns frequently outpunched Leonard, battered one eye closed, and was leading in the fourteenth round when Leonard uncorked a roundhouse right that rendered Hearns incoherent. Leonard shot both gloves into the air, his victory salute, and pounced on his foe to win by technical knockout. When they next fought, in 1989, I was in Costa Rica, having arrived ill after two days of revelry in Managua, Nicaragua. I had to take to my hotel bed most of the day, and arose late afternoon and entered the city of San Jose, looking for a place to watch the fight. I found a large and elegant restaurant, which turned out to be a cathouse I did not use in that capacity, and beseeched the manager to search for the fight on his cable network. Blessedly, he was able access it. As the superstars flailed each other for twelve rounds, I slurped locally-brewed beers and kept shouting, "La Guerra" – The War. After the armistice, judges called the fight a draw. Despite being a Leonard fan, I disagreed. Leonard also said Hearns deserved the decision.

Emanuel Steward culminated the 1980 interview by stating he preferred amateur boxing to professional, and noted, "Amateur boxing is making things come alive all over the country. Within two years I think you'll see eighty percent of the world professional titlists coming from the American amateur ranks."

In the decades since my conversation with Emanuel Steward, the base of boxing has narrowed as fans and top athletes focused on football, basketball, and other sports, including mixed martial arts, that provide faster and more fluid action than boxing. Steward continued to work with professional fighters at the pinnacle, as well as amateurs, but in free time he became a follower of mixed martial arts and was sometimes seen relaxing in a cage-side seat. That's the best place to be. Fighters too often have sad times. Tommy Hearns, after earning tens of millions of dollars in his career, lost his house and most valuable possessions due to debt he attributed to his "overly generous" aid to relatives. Gerald McClellan lost much more in 1995. He and Steward had just split over a financial dispute, and McClellan went to England to fight Nigel Benn. He knocked Benn out of the ring in the first round and down in the eighth but collapsed in the tenth and has since been blind and eighty percent deaf and must be cared for full-time. Even the professor of pugilism couldn't alter the consequences of a violent sport.

Editorial notes: Emanuel Steward died in October 2011. Ironically, or perhaps a realist would say predictably, many of his finest students can no longer speak well.

Death in the Ring

Alexis Arguello Explains

I am honored many people are calling me a legendary boxing champion who had a huge heart and danger in each hand, and even more I appreciate they consider me a kind and gracious gentleman. Still, I hear what some are asking, and feel what everyone's thinking: why couldn't Alexis, who persevered during many wars in the ring and a shooting war in the bush, keep going in everyday life? Though it is a private matter, I will tell you.

The pain was always there, even as a child. It was a pain in my mind and in my soul, and for many years I thought I suffered only because I was among the poorest people in Managua, Nicaragua and had to quit school at age nine and decided to run away from home to work on a farm. A year later I returned but still encountered only deprivation and vowed no more and at thirteen fled to a farm in Canada for a year, working to save money for my family. I returned with a thousand dollars, long hair, a tattoo on my arm, and the conviction I had to box to live.

After two years in the gym, I debuted in 1968 as a sixteen-year old with about a hundred twenty pounds stretched lean on my long, five-ten frame. A guy you'll never know stopped me in the first round. I was down but responded ambitiously, fighting as many as eleven times a year, sometimes every two or three weeks, always training and getting stronger and sharper, knocking out seven straight opponents and soon six more, not pausing after I was stopped again but rebounding with six KOs before winning a decision and then finishing another six.

In February 1974 I was ready for the featherweight title. It embodied the world I'd been living for – respect, money, homes, cars, and women – and Ernesto Marcel blocked my entrance. I pressured him fifteen rounds but that night the skillful champion punched faster and more accurately. Afterward, he promptly retired: few in boxing history have walked away with their titles, and none at age twenty-five.

I defeated four more opponents, three by knockout, before going to Los Angeles to challenge Ruben Olivares, the new featherweight titlist and Mexican king of America's most Mexican city. My team and I worried about the judges but needn't have: I pummeled Olivares, decked him twice in the thirteenth round, and became champion of the world. Several times I defended my crown and won many nontitle bouts, knocking out eleven of twelve opponents during one stretch and receiving more money and acclaim. I bought a beautiful home in Managua and then another and got a divorce and new wife and won my second world title in a bloody confrontation with super featherweight champion Alfredo Escalera.

Always I'd entered the ring in gentlemanly fashion, greeting my opponents, and afterward offered congratulations while checking to make sure they were all right. Nicaragua loved me and so did Latin America as well as boxing fans in the United States. The affection was gratifying but rarely relieved my pain. I knew a man should not be sad, and a world boxing champion must not express emotional pain. He must continue to beat up other men, and I did, knocking out past and future champions Bazooka Limon, Bobby Chacon, and Cornelius Boza Edwards. During this period I tried not to disintegrate when Sandinistas seized my homes, businesses, and bank accounts. What thugs they were. My brother had fought for them against dictator Anastasio Somoza's henchmen, who surrounded Eduardo on a Managua street before shooting him and torching his corpse on a pile of tires.

In the ring, I kept winning. My taut and slender frame amassed more muscle, and I moved up to one hundred thirty-five pounds, flew to London in 1981, and overpowered Jim Watt to earn a unanimous decision and the lightweight crown. Now I was one of few to have won three world championships. I also had my third wife, and children, and a home in Miami and a yacht nearby, but this was not enough. I needed an unprecedented fourth crown and the gorgeous women who helped me forget for a little while how I felt.

In Miami I would be facing Aaron Pryor, the junior welterweight champion, a muscular long-armed punching machine who'd defeated all thirty-three opponents, knocking out all but two, a ninety-four percent rate unmatched at the championship level. I wasn't afraid. I was going to destroy him. But he frequently landed first and I knew early I'd never been hit like that. I punished him, too, firing some of the hardest overhand rights of my career, haymakers that had felled many slightly smaller champions, but Pryor's jaw seemed reinforced by concrete. After the thirteenth round I felt I trailed but could win by capturing the final two rounds. Instead, Pryor erupted from his corner and bombarded me with two dozen power punches that crumpled me onto the canvas where for several minutes I lay, conscious but eyes closed, in a dreadful physical and emotional state.

At home I didn't want to leave the bedroom. My wife brought me food. My children, as ordered, stayed out. I was watching the video. For days I couldn't stop. I wanted to. And I should have. It made me sick. A younger, stronger, faster man was hitting me in the head and I did nothing but take it and now was so ashamed I didn't blame the referee for not stopping the fight a little sooner because I deserved punishment for failing so disgracefully. I plugged the tape back in, grimacing from each blow as I planned how to change things in the rematch. Sometimes I believed I could. A fighter must believe he can win. After two victories in ten months I was back in the ring with Aaron Pryor. In round ten he returned me to the canvas where I sat, knowing this man was better and I didn't want to box anymore.

My people and I had a more important war. Sandinistas still murdered and plundered, and I vowed to help defeat them. I wasn't a symbolic celebrity. I was a warrior who looked forward to being killed. Fatigues became my boxing shorts and a machine gun my fists. I wasn't going to wait long. Without orders three dozen Contras and I decided to annihilate a Sandinista village stronghold. As we silently approached, an enemy spotted us and began firing and others responded too, hitting one of my friends, and I sprayed bullets before running to get him amid enemy fire ripping earth while my Contras screamed leave him he's dead.

They wanted an immaculate war offering much leisure time in their elegant Costa Rican homes. And they wanted to ignore Indians suffering from starvation and dysentery. They're going to die, I warned. Medicine and supplies are for the Contras, I was told. I don't like you or your war, I said, and returned to Managua then Miami and a house my wife had abandoned because of my excesses. Please come back, I urged. I can't lose you and the kids too.

They returned but couldn't help. I snorted cocaine until my nose bled and my mind screamed then snorted more and drank alcohol to come down as well as prepare for the next blast. In 1984, on my yacht The Champ, I looked into eternal relief, the barrel of a loaded pistol. My eldest son pleaded don't do it. I cried I had to. I'd thrown away all my money, my homes, perhaps my health and my family, and the IRS wanted more. I needed out, yet somehow didn't pull the trigger. Boxing might keep me alive. In my 1985 comeback I fought the first time since the second Pryor fight and won by technical knockout against a quality opponent and duplicated that the following year. I was probably still better than anyone my size except Aaron Pryor.

I could have continued, though I frequently felt the eighteen-year accumulation of punches. Why did I need boxing? I was studying acting because many told me I had the swarthy, mustachioed look of a Latin lover. And I promoted young fighters and battled for medical insurance and pensions for boxers who needed help. I also provided live commentary during televised matches and planned businesses and sports camps but kept staying out late, often all night, and by 1994 had drifted too far and needed money so at age forty-two I reentered the ring against a pug with two wins and twelve losses, a guy I earlier would've promptly destroyed, and for ten rounds struggled to scrape out a decision. The following year I fought a man who could hit back and he beat me by unanimous decision. There was no point continuing, not as a fighter.

As a man battered by fists, finances, and another divorce, I went home to Nicaragua. Everywhere I stepped I was still a hero, the most popular and revered man in the country, and I dedicated myself to helping people. I became involved in political issues. I tackled social problems. The appreciation I received was overwhelming. And before long I picked up a pistol and considered shooting myself. People said I was using cocaine again. If so, it was to treat my depression.

There must've been better treatment. I sought it in 2004 when I ran for Vice Mayor of Managua. To help me campaign I brought in Aaron Pryor, my old conqueror but now good friend. People roared and I was elected and felt great being a champion again. Political enemies later accused me of misappropriating funds for pork barrel projects and building a personal home. These charges I denied. In the summer of 2008 I bore my nation's flag during the opening ceremony of the Olympics. Then in November I ran for Mayor of Managua. President Daniel Ortega, who long ago had been a far more dangerous nemesis than Pryor, now supported me as a fellow Sandinista. Crowds grew even larger, and in open vehicles I stood, celebrity and leader, and waved to cheering supporters lining the streets. They needed me but not nearly so much as I needed them. I was hospitalized that month with an undisclosed ailment many surmised they knew. Thankfully, I won a close election.

I was very proud despite some domestic and international charges Sandinistas had used fraud and intimidation to engineer victory. There was nothing unusual about this Nicaraguan election. I committed myself to the people and tried to ignore stress. On June twenty-sixth, 2009 I had the privilege of flying to Puerto Rico to honor Roberto Clemente, the Pittsburgh Pirate hall of famer who in December 1972 died trying to fly supplies to Managua where an earthquake had killed five thousand people and leveled much of the city. I gave a moving speech and placed a wreath on the great man's grave. A little more than four days later, early in the morning of July first, in my Managua home, I placed a high-caliber pistol against my heart and left my face intact for family and nation.

George Thomas Clark

Lennox Lewis Retires

One of the best heavyweight champions in history retired last week. Not many noticed; even fewer thought it a milestone to be celebrated; no one seemed very emotional about the end of Lennox Lewis' fourteen-year professional career during which he lost only twice, reversed both setbacks, and dominated the big men's division for several years. Saying farewell now, in 2004, Lewis thus becomes only the third heavyweight to leave with his title. Gene Tunney, during the Coolidge administration, was the first. Rocky Marciano, almost fifty years ago, had been the last. Both were justifiably praised not merely for being undefeated champions but as shrewd gentlemen who departed before they had to be carried out of the ring. Lewis, on the contrary, is being dismissed by many as a minor heavyweight champion who failed to thrill the masses. Even Lewis' sometime trainer, Emanuel Steward, publicly complained before big fights that his winning by decision or unexciting knockout wouldn't be good enough.

Of course it wouldn't. What boxing fans really want is to watch one man destroy another or, even better, two men demolishing each other. Brace yourself and look at Muhammad Ali, the ultimate warrior and once incomparable talker. He can't really speak anymore. But that's okay. He and Joe Frazier gave us Super Fight I, an astonishing display of power and brutality. And they tripled that violence in Super Fight III, the Thrilla in Manila, the greatest prize fight ever. Muhammad Ali, the Louisville Lip, the king of glib, the charismatic young Cassius, can't take care of himself anymore. And before the third Frazier fight, he'd beaten big George Foreman in the Rumble in the Jungle and won his title back. He should have quit then like Lewis is now. Instead, he fought Kenny Norton a third time, and Norton continued to pound Ali as he had in their first two fights. Then Ali ate numerous right hand bombs from powerful Earnie Shavers. Later in his heroic charge into invalidism, Ali, in a strategic sense, gave away his title by leaning back on the ropes and letting an overmatched Leon Spinks flail him for fifteen rounds. Then he won the title back – his third – and should have stepped (by then rather feebly) away. But he preferred to go out on his shield, and he did. Larry Holmes carved him up. In boxing, the more extreme the suffering, the greater is the celebration of the hero.

Lennox Lewis never wanted to be a hero badly enough to completely sacrifice his body. He wasn't going to be bloody meat for the salivating spectators at the Colosseum. Instead, he was going to win fights scientifically, using his six-foot-five frame and enormous reach to pound people from afar with jabs and overhand rights. He was going to beat them like the superpower beats people with bombs and missiles. As safe and far away as possible, that's what he wanted. In boxing, that's not sufficiently dramatic. So after beating Vitali Klitschko, a skillful young giant from Ukraine, Lennox Lewis, one of the best who ever entered a ring, is stepping out, rich and healthy. But, according to many of those beer-swilling studs at ringside, what Lewis achieved was ultimately pretty damn disappointing.

George Thomas Clark

Letters to Three Boxers

Dear Riddick Bowe,

I'm writing to you first, in the fall of 2004, because I feel your circumstances are the most critical. You were a splendid fighter, unusually big and strong and hard-hitting even by the standards of heavyweight champions, and you gave ravenous boxing fans three memorable wars with Evander Holyfield. In fact, you were the only man to knock out Holyfield when he was in his prime. But you were hurt more then than we realized. It soon became evident when Andrew Golota, the big Pole, twice gave you dreadful beatings and lost only because he couldn't stop hitting below your belt. The Riddick Bowe who twice conquered Holyfield would have dominated, and probably knocked out, Golota. But I'm not writing you about your performance in the ring.

I'm writing about your health. You, who used to imitate the glib young Ali so well, began to slur your words. In that sense, ironically, you were following the sad decline of the great man. Your impaired speech, of course, wasn't the only sign of what some doctors diagnosed as brain damage. You also kidnapped your children and former wife and did time in prison for it. Yet you recently claimed the doctors "said crazy things like I was punchy. They're the ones who are punchy." That's analogous to a man who's had several heart attacks claiming his surgeon needs a bypass.

Evidently, your condition has at least temporarily improved, and it's wonderful that you're again a free man. What is most alarming, however, is your insistence on returning to the ring. Your former manager, Rock Newman, was appalled and said he couldn't imagine anyone licensing a thirty-seven-year old in your condition to fight. It's doubtful officials in Nevada, the current capital of boxing, would have let you step into any ring after the bell rang. But in the dirty business of boxing there's always someone to pay a guy to give and take a beating, even a man who's a mere punch removed from incontinence or worse. For you, the chance to return to combat came on an Indian reservation in Oklahoma.

The Associated Press wrote about the spectacle, and with apparent relief noted: "Some in boxing were worried Riddick Bowe would get hurt making a comeback after eight years outside the ring. (But) he was the one doing the hurting." That, on a superficial level, is true. Despite weighing about 40 pounds more than you should, and refusing to step on the scales to certify that, you pounded a guy who's paid to get knocked out and who himself shouldn't be in the ring. You didn't come back to fight under-qualified members of the pugilistic world, though. You returned for big fights and big bucks and lots of attention. And to get those things you'll have to challenge very dangerous young men in their prime. I hope that won't happen. I'm not questioning your punching power. No doubt, you still have that. And I don't care if you can win fights, though I'm convinced you can't beat any top contender. I'm talking about your brain. If you take many more punches there won't be any more recoveries. Your health will be gone forever. Do the smart thing. Stay out of the ring unless you're a distinguished former champion waving to the crowd before someone else's main event.

Dear Roy Jones,

When a boxer like you beats everyone he fights for more than a decade, usually dominating opponents while minimizing punishment received, most observers don't worry or even think about the champion's health. The well-being of his opponents seems to be the urgent issue. Unbeaten fighters – I'm not counting your 1997 disqualification as a loss, when you decked a guy after the bell – frequently seem like they'll be forever invincible. That's how it's been with you. Everyone who follows boxing knew that. No middleweight could challenge you, then you moved up to super middleweight, then light heavyweight, and none of those guys were threatening, either. And year after year, almost everyone acknowledged it: "Roy Jones is the finest pound for pound fighter in the world."

You proved that and more in March 2003. Since last fighting, you built eighteen pounds of muscle on a frame you still maneuvered with remarkable speed and agility against two hundred twenty-six pound WBA heavyweight champion John Ruiz, who'd defeated Evander Holyfield. And you did more than most imagined: you knocked down a much bigger man and won by four, six, and eight rounds on the official cards. In deference to Lennox Lewis, far the best heavyweight champion for several years, we must acknowledge you couldn't have beaten, nor would you have tried to beat, such an enormous and talented opponent.

But that didn't matter. You were boxing royalty, a successor to the kings of multiple-title acquisition – Henry Armstrong, Sugar Ray Robinson, Roberto Duran, Sugar Ray Leonard, Tommy Hearns, and Michael Spinks. Then you did the most astonishing thing. You decided to burn off those eighteen pounds of muscle and slide back down to the light heavyweight division, where you'd also lost much of your enthusiasm for the competition. The first result, in November 2003, was not encouraging. You lacked your customary strength and stamina while winning a close and controversial majority decision over Antonio Tarver. Several months later Tarver nailed you with a perfect counter left hook – "right on the kisser," he said – and you were in an unfamiliar place, on the canvas being counted out. You said you could have continued. It's understandable you felt that way. But last Saturday, after Glen Johnson hammered you with a right-left combination, you lay almost motionless on the deck for four minutes. Your handlers, so recently accustomed to raising your hand, had to gently lift your head to place ice underneath. Eventually, you were aided in walking out of the ring.

You have won many fights, Roy. You have humbled many men. Now you must look at the most recent results and see yourself as you used to see your opponents. You are now the one in danger. Counting your amateur career, you have at least two decades of ring wars on your resume, and, more importantly, carved into your brain. There is no way to deny its time to quit. Perhaps you've already acknowledged that. If you haven't, do so soon, and concentrate on your burgeoning career as a ringside color commentator, and play some hoops. That sport keeps mind and body clear and strong.

Death in the Ring

Dear Oscar De La Hoya,

I hope you've read the two letters above and will talk to Riddick and Roy. You might be the best guy in the world to do so. You can tell them you understand the thrill and gratification of being a world champion, and that contemplating life without boxing is painful. None of you, after all, will ever have such intense excitement again. I've also asked you to talk to them because I assume you're not going to fight much longer. You've always seemed much too shrewd and calculating to hang around until you can only take beatings. Surely you're not going to do that. You want to retain that stellar face. And you should. Women aren't the only ones who talk about it, you know. Even men comfortably comment about your nice features.

But most of all, Oscar, you need to protect your brain. You're thirty-one and have been fighting since you were a kid. The punches you took then still count now. I'm sure you know that. More recently, you've learned you cannot beat a superb middleweight champion. Bernard Hopkins knocked you out with one shot to the body. It must've been about a century since a major title fight was decided by a single punch downstairs. That would be when Bob Fitzsimmons crumpled "Gentleman" Jim Corbett with his famous uppercut to the solar plexus. The bigger and stronger Hopkins took you out with a left hook to the liver.

You've won every world title from junior lightweight to junior middleweight, a hundred thirty to a hundred fifty-four pounds, but you have maxed out. You're not a middleweight, and there aren't any more titles you can win, are there? You've made not merely scores but hundreds of millions of dollars and long been an international celebrity. So for you, too, Oscar, it is almost time to leave. In your case it would not be imprudent to have one more fight, a third and final shot at Shane Mosley, your hometown LA rival who's twice beaten you. The decisions were close but clear cut. The fans understand you want him. You probably want him badly enough to give him what he demands and has earned – the larger end of the purse. You're the bigger star, but the precise number of millions you'd make won't be the deciding issue. You want redemption. Go for it.

But, please – before and after your next and final fight – stress your determination to get out before you get hurt. And make sure to urge Riddick Bowe and Roy Jones to retire at once.

Sincerely,

GTC

Death in the Ring

The Fifth Pacquiao-Marquez War

I am honored that promoters, commissioners, and, indeed, Manny Pacquiao and Juan Manuel Marquez have hired me to oversee the inevitable fifth war between two indefatigable boxers who've been campaigning for a generation. Contracts have not yet been signed but they will be. Though the opening round of their first fight, several years ago, featured Pacquiao thrice knocking down Marquez, their initial three meetings were more scientific than compelling and only a dearth of other pugilistic options compelled lusty fans to jam a casino arena in Las Vegas and huddle around pay-per-view televisions worldwide to watch what many considered a superfluous fourth confrontation. Thankfully, these boxers understood they were gladiators, not elusive bullfighters, and for weeks vowed to batter each other and so did from opening bell.

Pacquiao seemed quicker and stronger until the third round when Marquez decked him with a roundhouse right launched from Reno. Pacquiao arose and recovered, resumed his offensive by the fifth round, knocked Marquez down with a left cross, landed numerous other power punches, broke his opponent's nose, bloodied his mouth, and continued pressure in the sixth up to the final second when he lunged at Marquez and ate a right-hand hammer that rendered the formerly indestructible Manny unconscious before he landed, horrifically, nose down and motionless on the canvas. While Marquez climbed the ropes to celebrate for himself and all of Mexico, the beautiful Mrs. Pacquiao, who'd often urged her husband to forsake boxing, and even threatened to leave him over the issue, became tearful and traumatized as she tried to enter the ring to help.

Modest Marquez downplayed his many large new muscles, rare achievements for an elite athlete at age thirty-nine, and said quickness was the main reason for victory. Once he awakened, Pacquiao, bruised but less so than Marquez, said he wanted another chance. Since Marquez was out-earned in this fight perhaps three to one, around eighteen million to six, he'll be eager to earn at least twice as much to fight a once-larger man now smaller than he.

That's the issue I'm hired to address. Let's admit it. Battered opponents of Manny Pacquiao, now thirty-four-years old, often said it was impossible for a man then in his late twenties and early thirties to gain so much weight and muscle while maintaining speed and the ability to relentlessly attack. Now the middle-aged Marquez is accused of the same biochemical indiscretions, and displeased that his muscle growth is being likened to that of once-sleek outfielder Barry Bonds who became Herculean at age thirty-seven and hit seven-three homers in one season, after generally needing two years to hit that many. In their first three fights, Marquez many times landed strong rights to Pacquiao's head yet had never knocked him down. Now he's annihilated him with a single shot. Granted, Pacquiao moved into the punch and, certainly, his skills have eroded. But my concern is that Pacquiao may have quit taking performance enhancing drugs or at least hadn't been taking as many as Marquez.

This injustice I shall not allow to continue. My mandate is this: gentlemen, you are hereby ordered to take the best drugs and you are to take precisely the same amounts of the same boosters. In order to enforce compliance, you will be confined to the same Alcatraz training facility throughout preparations for Fight Five. This is not outrageous. It's farsighted and humane. We cannot and will not risk either of you being under-drugged or, more frighteningly, drug free the next time you meet. That would be too damn dangerous.

Emergency Evaluation of a Judge

After Floyd Mayweather jabbed, right crossed, dodged, entangled and tormented poor young Canelo Alvarez for twelve rounds, all viewers waited to hear whether flashy Floyd had officially won every round or only about nine to earn a six-point victory. Ring announcer Jimmy Lennon, Jr., then revealed this Las Vegas extravaganza would be decided by majority decision. We evidently misunderstood the distinguished voice, or perhaps this was a ruse by his late father, speaking from the hereafter and injecting his nearly identical vocal tones into the mouth of his son. Lennon, the one standing in the ring and presumably providing serious and accurate information, thereupon told us that one of the judges had scored the fight 114-114. He just as credibly could've announced he was in Timbuktu. Let us credit Mayweather for not extending knuckles and diving onto the judges' table. Alvarez also earns praise for suppressing laughter, for even he would've scored the fight decisively for Mayweather, and in gentlemanly tones soon said so.

Anger evaporated as most realized that no boxing judge could be so incompetent or hateful. Indeed, such an appalling decision must have resulted from a medical malady. Members of the august Nevada Athletic Commission, accompanied by surgeons and emergency medical technicians, engulfed the three judges and demanded: who did this? The other two pointed at Cynthia J. Ross, who must possess a secret that frightens powerful people in blistering Las Vegas. How else could she have earned eight grand to sit at ringside and judge a major event? Isn't this the same Cynthia J. Ross who decreed that Manny Pacquiao lost to Timothy Bradley because, evidently, Pacquiao landed eighty percent more power punches? Yes, it's the same person. But Ross had an ally, another disturbed arbiter, in the Pacquiao fight and, though stink-inducing, the decision was not appalling enough to mandate immediate intervention.

Floyd Mayweather's handling of Canelo Alvarez was entirely more serious. If Alvarez landed even a single strong punch, most observers missed it. If he scored with more than a half dozen decent shots, no one but Cynthia J. Ross noticed. Mayweather after the fight was sore in only two spots, his left fist which frequently jabbed the face of Alvarez, and his right which he used to hammer his opponent's head. Medical experts agreed Ross had to be examined at once. She was tested for alcohol – negative. She was tested for all manner of uppers – negative. She was tested for powerful painkillers – negative. She was tested for hallucinogens – negative. She was given a visual exam and identified most letters on the chart. Her bank account was checked to see if a few million had recently rolled in. That hadn't happened, either. What could it be? How could a professional judge mistake a decision so overwhelming it's entirely objective rather than subjective, one so obvious every kid on a playground would accurately assess?

Doctors still don't know, so the FBI will conduct the next examination.

Letter to Oscar De La Hoya

Dear Oscar,

I'm sorry to learn you're back in rehab but glad you went. Most alcoholics never submit to inpatient treatment. I never did but should have during three decades of excess. I've read enough about you to conclude you probably didn't drink and use daily. Neither did I, and that's how I so long justified it: I only do it on weekends. Right, people said, you're wacked out two days and then need two more to recover.

Now I'm approaching sixteen years of sobriety, a feat no one imagined, so I'd like to offer some things I learned. Alcoholics are usually nervous people and often depressed. If the latter is true, daily prayers to a higher power will not be enough to sustain sobriety. I'm not suggesting you run and get a psychiatrist, if you haven't already, but I am guaranteeing that a large slice of alcoholics are undermined by brains naturally hyper and anxious, and people in pain will seek medication. Look at history. Glance around your AA meetings: how many people have ten or more years sobriety, and how many have less than thirty days? Those answers won't be encouraging. At least you have a better chance than poor alcoholics, who likely won't have the opportunity to undergo rehab or consult experts in psychopharmacology.

I'll make a few suggestions regarding slippery situations. No one can eliminate all of them, but you can erase most. First, don't keep alcohol in your home. You can't handle it, and your guests don't need it. Sober alcoholics learn, often to their surprise, that most people either don't drink or drink damn little. Avoid those who think drinking is obligatory and fun. They'll ruin themselves, and they'll help you ruin yourself. Also, stay out of bars and nightclubs. And don't claim you've got to be there for business. Bullshit. You're the Golden Boy worth a hundred fifty million bucks. Do your business socializing in wholesome restaurants or private homes. Make a list of where you were and how you felt the last several times you lurched off the wagon. You'll see handwritten confirmation of what you already know.

If AA works for you, great. The fellowship has helped millions of people save themselves and others from self-destruction. Though I learned much at AA meetings, I may be biased against them since I never reached thirty days sobriety during the two years or so I regularly attended. For me, the unrelenting "war stories" about drinking and drug taking and the sordid tales of domestic violence, divorce, poverty, jail and death were depressing and actually made me dwell on drinking and using more than I otherwise would have. Of course, I did need the learning and support, or I wouldn't have been advised and eventually compelled to attend meetings.

It's better I simply say, stay with AA, Oscar. Since after drinking you often charge toward cocaine, a sequence I regrettably understand, then you must do everything to avoid taking that first drink because, as all alcoholics should know, "one drink is too many and a thousand are never enough." And we can add that alcohol isn't enough, either. One night of cocaine can blow out any heart, and the places users have to go to get it are rife with bullets and bad people. I'm confident you already know you will die well before old age if you continue drinking and using. Like many, I wonder how I survived until I established permanent sobriety, at age forty-five. Only luck, the empty chamber in a recurring game of Russian roulette, saves people who abuse. Those are wretched odds in a degrading process. So throw away the gun forever. And good luck.

Sincerely,

GTC

Angelo Dundee Advises Adrien Broner

Son, you're urinating some blood and getting your jaw looked at, but you'll be okay, unless you fight too long. People better not celebrate your loss to Marcos Maidana too much. I know what happened. You overestimated yourself. You're not the next Floyd Mayweather or Sugar Ray Leonard but maybe you can still be better than everyone else your size, when Floyd retires or forgets to leave. Your bad manners aren't helping but they aren't the other problem, weight is. You're not really a welterweight yet. Seventeen months ago you were fighting as a junior lightweight, just ten months ago you were a lightweight and way too slim. Right now a hundred forty-seven's a shade too big. You need to get a little bigger and a lot stronger. Maidana taught you that, sort of like Duran showed Leonard in their first fight. But remember, Leonard didn't go down, and left hooks twice put you on the canvas. You also got up twice and landed solid punches and won some rounds. You were beaten but not destroyed. Look at the twelfth round. You were still strong and competitive. But you couldn't dominate. You thought your jab would bust up a guy who'd lost three times, and you planned to hit him with combinations any time you wanted. His power taught you the truth.

Like I said, you've got to get stronger at welterweight or go down to one-forty, only a few pounds less than you weighed this fight. I say stay at welterweight and build yourself up in that division. You were destroying the little guys but only got a split decision over Paulie Malignaggi your first fight as a welter. Then you ran into a bull from Argentina who didn't care about your mouth or your punch. Don't take a rematch right away against this guy. After you heal, and that'll be a few months, fight a couple of solid welterweights. Work on your power punching. Tighten up your left hook. Sometimes you're almost slapping. Also, work on lateral movement. In the eighth round your hands were up when Maidana nailed you with a left hook that actually hurt you more than the one that soon knocked you down. You're not Floyd on defense. Forget that. You've got to move side to side, son. And when you stop you've got to be the one who puts guys on the deck. If you do these things, you'll be much better than against Madiana, and he'll be a little older. He's a tough guy but will never be that good again. Really, he did you a favor. He showed what it takes to be a welterweight champion. I don't think you'll have any more illusions. One more thing, put away the damn video camera until you grow up.

Editorial note: Boxing fans know, but others probably do not, that Adrien Broner has voluntarily been filmed defecating in a public restroom and copulating with a moaning prostitute.

Final Days of Teofilo Stevenson

In my adult ESL class dominated by students from Mexico I heard a different accent and in Spanish asked, "Where are you from?"

"Cuba," he said.

"Too bad Teofilo Stevenson died so young, only sixty."

"He had alcohol and drug problems, and many problems with women, too."

"Really?"

"Sí."

I was stunned. I hadn't envisioned Teofilo Stevenson as a man who'd have major problems. Instead his name always evoked images of a man tall and strong, swift and graceful who glided in the rings of international amateur boxing as he patiently left jabbed opponents, and waited, knowing what many of his targets surely sensed. There'd be an opening at the side of a head or on a jaw, and like an automated weapon, too fast to avoid and too powerful to withstand, the right hand of Teofilio Stevenson would fire and crumple those before him.

In the 1972 Olympics Duane Bobick, the favorite who'd decisioned nineteen-year-old Stevenson the year before, was knocked into a fetal position on the canvas. In the 1976 Olympics a single right finished John Tate, who slumped in a corner. Stevenson captured his third gold medal in 1980 when the United States boycotted the Games to protest the Soviet Union's invasion of Afghanistan. He likewise won the World Amateur Championship three times, highlighted by his decision over Tony Tubbs and right-hand bombing of Alex Garcia. He also tripled his titles in the Pan American Games where in 1975 he defeated Michael Dokes.

So impressive was Teofilo Stevenson that most observers considered him a likely professional champion, if he wanted to be so. Tony Tubbs, Michael Dokes, and John Tate would proceed to win portions of the heavyweight title. Duane Bobick and Alex Garcia forged solid professional careers. Stevenson's fans, particularly in communist countries, shouted that he would also beat Muhammad Ali, he'd hammer George Foreman, he'd dominate Larry Holmes. To those boasts I must say: hold it, Stevenson fought only men when they were amateurs and never did so more than three rounds, after which many pros are just breaking a sweat. Also, Igor Vysotsky, a stocky Russian slugger but not pro-caliber contender, outpointed Stevenson in 1973 and stopped him three years later. To win the heavyweight championship of the free world, Teofilo Stevenson would've had to fight up to fifteen rounds against the speed and toughness of Ali and Holmes. He would've had to withstand Foreman blows more powerful than those of Vysotsky. He would've had to stand on the grandest stage.

Stevenson said he cared not for the money or Westernized glory offered him by Don King and other carnies, and we must believe him. He certainly had opportunities to defect at many locations around the world, but that would've taken him far from the love of several million Cubans whose feelings, he emphasized, mattered most to him. But what else touched Stevenson, a man who had more than three hundred amateur fights and fought thousands of rounds in the gym. How did those ring skirmishes affect him? We don't know what he would've been like without receiving countless blows to the head, but boxing history is rife with men who behaved badly during and after their careers.

Not long before Teofilo Stevenson died in June 2012, a man called Brin-Jonathan Butler privately paid Stevenson – not the Cuban government – a hundred fifty dollars for seventy-five minutes of his time on camera. Butler warily entered the gate through walls that surrounded Stevenson's modest home, a gift from noted sports director Fidel Castro. Some people in Havana said wives – Stevenson divorced four times – and girlfriends occasionally had to escape over the walls or through the gate. In 1999 the slugger certifiably head-butted and broke some teeth of an airline ticket employee in Miami. Stevenson said he was harassed. The employee swore otherwise. Stevenson, then a boxing official, returned to Cuba with the team and never revisited the United States.

Brin-Jonathan Butler wrote that when he arrived, early in the morning, Stevenson was already intoxicated and drinking vodka from a water bottle. He was also smoking and, during the interview, demanded a couple of cigarette breaks, camera off but the clock running. When questioning resumed Stevenson stated that he did not regret declining to turn pro and fight Ali. How could he have fought the great Ali? Look at the picture of the two comrades on

Stevenson's wall. Ali is shrunken into a pugilistic Parkinson's shell of incontinence and virtually unrecognizable as the beautiful athlete he'd been. How could we have fought, Stevenson asked? We're brothers. If you imagine the young Ali superimposed over the old one, the men do look alike, as Stevenson, too, was a magnificent man.

Did he have any regrets?

Inhaling a cigarette, swigging more vodka, gray and skinny Teofilo Stevenson said, "Do I look like I regret any decision I've made? I have no regrets, I'm the happiest man in the world. And our time is up."

Smokin' Joe

In epic fights one and three Smokin' Joe Frazier hurled left hooks about destroying Muhammad Ali who countered with cutting right hands in a ring neither should've entered. Several years after their final clash silence enveloped Ali but humble Joe Frazier declared revenge for his foe's unforgotten insults. Decades later and weak himself Frazier still celebrated those special nights rocking the world with Muhammad Ali. Now Smokin' Joe's gone and a quiet man feebly stands mourning his rival on some level aware they fought too well.

Cassius Clay Again

I've got nothing to prove. I've beaten the unbeatable Sonny Liston twice and am the undefeated heavyweight champion of the world. I'm only twenty-three and tired of fighting, been doing it since I was twelve. I'm too pretty to fight anymore. I'm too clever to let men pound my brain. I'm going into politics. I'm going to be a civil rights leader. I know people will say I'm crazy to retire so young. They'll say I won't be able to stay away. They'll say I'm a fool. They're wrong. I'm going to knock out racism. I'm going to flatten poverty. I'm going to win civil rights for my people. I'm going to help end the war in Vietnam. Those opponents are more fearsome than all heavyweight contenders combined. I'll stay motivated. I'll still get up early and run a few miles and shadow box several rounds. I'll always have that rush. Then I'll go into neighborhoods, churches, and schools, and I'll recite poems and kiss babies and give speeches and occasionally dance a little and throw some punches. And when the next generation of heavyweights calls me chicken, I'll ask what they've done today and are planning to do tomorrow. And how do their heads feel? That's what I'll say.

George Thomas Clark

Jerry Quarry from Boxers' Heaven

I'm Jerry Quarry and I hope you've heard about me. I was the top ranked heavyweight contender and knew I'd soon be champion of the world. Boxing fans, women, television crews, and promoters with money all wanted me, and I loved my bright days of dreams and glory. But I don't miss them anymore. They led to a long and undignified decline. Now I'm much better off in Shafter Memorial Park, a pretty place with lots of big trees about twenty miles northwest of Bakersfield. And it just got better here Saturday when they brought the ashes of my kid brother Mike, who'd been the top ranked light heavyweight contender in the world. We're together again and will be forever, here by the railroad tracks and Central Valley Highway that run through this hot farming country our family left when we were kids.

We moved to Bellflower, a suburb southeast of Los Angeles, and in no time they were calling me the Bellflower Bomber. I'd been made for that. My tough dad Jack had Hard Luck tattooed on his knuckles and threw all four brothers into the ring soon as possible and told us to keep swinging no matter what since "there's no quit in a Quarry." Jimmy was the oldest and the only man to really knock me down for the count. I was just thirteen and he was fourteen, and a year's a lot when you're a kid, so that knockout didn't mean much. Besides, Jimmy, unlike my other brothers, decided not to go for a pro career since I was soon pounding him so hard he knew he'd never even be champ of our family.

I was definitely going to be champion of the world. I had more than two hundred amateur fights and of course fought thousands of training rounds in the gym. I didn't think of it then, feeling invincible, but punches in those days also counted. Your brain doesn't care how young you are; it only knows it's bashing against a skull being hammered from outside. I thought I was the only one doing real damage. While still a teenager I won the National Golden Gloves title by knocking out five straight opponents. No one had done that and no one's done it since.

Dad said I should turn pro and I did and beat up almost everyone and never lost except a close decision to veteran Eddie Machen and didn't bother fighting him again because by age twenty-two I'd been selected for the tournament to decide who would replace Muhammad Ali as champ after he was banished in 1967 for refusing to join the army. In the first fight I decisioned former titlist Floyd Patterson and in the next I stopped contender Thad Spencer. Then I fought Jimmy Ellis for the heavyweight championship of the world. I knew damn well I won but the referee and one judge said Ellis did; the other referee called it a draw. That wouldn't matter for long.

Within a year I'd knocked out three more boxers and decisioned two and earned a shot at part of the title against Joe Frazier. And the fight was in the greatest place of all – Madison Square Garden. I came right after Smokin' Joe and nailed him with left hooks and right crosses to the head and also battered his body in round one and now I really knew I was best in the world and Frazier couldn't take many more punches. I continued attacking but Frazier began hitting me with left hooks harder than anything I'd imagined, and I was groggy and cut and bleeding fast. They were going to do it. They were going to deny me again. They said the cut was too bad for me to continue. I protested like hell.

That's really where it should have ended. I can say that now. Joe Frazier was better, and I feared, no matter what I said, that I was never going to win the world title. Six months later plodding but powerful George Chuvalo knocked me out. The hell he did. I didn't hear the count. The referee didn't count right. I could've gotten up before ten. I think I might have. It was close. It was another big loss. But there's no quit in a Quarry. In June 1970 I was still only twenty-five and returning to Madison Square Garden. My opponent was a big heavyweight – they were all bigger since I weighed less than two hundred pounds – named Mac Foster who'd won all twenty-four fights by knockout. And I knocked his ass out. Again I knew I was the best anywhere and ready to prove it that October when Muhammad Ali made his comeback following more than three years in exile. I knew I could've beaten him. I was just cut again. He was lucky. But looking at the film now, as I should have then, I see Ali was much too big and fast for me. I should've been fighting as a cruiserweight but they didn't have that division. There was only the light heavyweight division with a limit of one seventy-five or heavyweight and no limit.

I wasn't worried. I beat six guys in less than two years and in 1972 got a rematch with Ali. This was a very special night: "The Quarry Brothers versus the Soul Brothers." My little brother Mike, only twenty-one years old, had won his first thirty-six light heavyweight bouts and was fighting for the title against Bob Foster in the opener. I was more nervous for Mike than myself. Bob Foster was one of the hardest-hitting light heavies ever. Mike was a skillful boxer but not a knockout puncher. From the start Foster overpowered him, punching like a heavyweight. Mike was still game and trying to win in the fourth round when he stepped in and Foster uncorked the best left hook in a lifetime of great ones and nailed Mike on the chin, knocking him cold on his back. That scared hell out of me.

I was going to kill Ali. In our bout I charged and picked him up and guess I shouldn't have put him down because when I did he was still far larger and quicker, and busted me up when he wasn't toying with me. They stopped the fight in the seventh round. I wish Mike and I had both quit after that night. Maybe we'd be home instead of Shafter Memorial Park. But Mike and I were talented and handsome and Irish and everyone wanted to see us in the ring. That's the only place we'd ever really been. I knew I should continue. Ask Ron Lyle. In 1973 he was undefeated and thought he was getting a title tune-up by taking me on in Madison Square Garden. He instead got a boxing lesson as I slipped most of his punches and punished him with counters and staggered him a few times, winning unanimously. A few months later, also in The Garden, I fought one of the most dreaded punchers in history, the man with the right-hand bomb, Earnie Shavers. He didn't make it out of the first round.

Understandably, I again felt destined to win the title. Joe Frazier was next. He'd be a stepping stone to the new champ, George Foreman. I wasn't going to get unlucky this time. There was really no luck about it. Frazier's left hook almost tore out my right eye. I have no idea why I didn't quit then. I gave it one more try against a major opponent in 1975, and muscular Ken Norton ripped my face. Now everyone, even trainers and promoters, said I should quit. And I did, intensifying my alcohol and cocaine abuse and rough domestic style that eventually resulted in three marriages and divorces, before coming back two years later. I looked horrible until finally nailing a weak-jawed Italian and then quit again until 1983 when I beat two guys who couldn't fight much. The scariest news came when Sports Illustrated published cognitive medical tests showing I'd suffered irreversible brain damage and had dementia pugilistica, which meant I was punch drunk and would become more so. They concluded the same about renowned brawler Bobby Chacon. I said the medical testers could wipe their butts with the article. And I would ignore them again. At age forty-seven in 1992, wanting to launch a comeback in middle-age like George Foreman, I, who'd earned a couple of million dollars in my career, accepted a thousand bucks to take on a guy who couldn't have touched me in my prime but knocked me around the ring for six rounds. The next day I didn't remember what happened.

It was way too late by then. When was it too late for my brother Mike? I suppose no talented twenty-one year old is going to retire, even after a brutal knockout loss to Bob Foster. Mike kept fighting and beating most opponents and lost only decisions to top guys. In his corner I wasn't alarmed until the third time he fought Mike Rossman, in 1977. Two years earlier he'd decisioned Rossman. The following year Rossman reversed that. Now my brother was battered and stopped in the sixth round and afterward I screamed at him, "Say it. Say it." Say you won't fight anymore. It may already have been too late, but maybe not.

There's no quit in a Quarry. Mike fought five more years and, counting his Rossman fights, lost six of his last twelve including four by knockout. That's really what happens when fighters don't quit. We take beatings and our damaged brains start grinding out unintelligible sounds delivered by thick tongues. Soon after leaving the ring we shuffle like men in their eighties and can't work even menial jobs or recall what we did this morning and at night we hear voices that make us scream. While our brains continue to shrink fast, we need to be cared for like babies and eventually we can't walk or talk at all and our dead brains shut down our breathing. Imagine, that was my life until I came to Shafter Memorial Park in 1999. That was Mike's life and that of others who have the same unknowing gaze I had the 1995 night I was inducted into the Boxing Hall of Fame. I wish I'd really known I was there.

I wish Muhammad Ali hadn't fought so much he got pugilistic

Parkinson's and lost his speaking ability so long ago I was able to note in an interview: "It's a guarantee he's not the guy he was." I wish I hadn't insisted I was fine. I wasn't any more than my former opponents Floyd Patterson, who just died from boxing-induced Alzheimer's disease, and incoherent Jimmy Ellis. It's also too late for paralyzed Greg Page, a once large and fast heavyweight contender who was critically injured at age forty-one while fighting in a dump that lacked proper medical equipment. Page died a few years later. I pray it's not too late for my youngest brother Bobby, who didn't fight nearly as long as the guys above but still has suffered nerve damage in his brain. That's probably why he's in prison and had to get a special one-day pass to come to Mike's memorial service.

Bad as it is, maybe we were the lucky ones. Lots of guys died soon after being carried from the ring. Duk-Koo Kim and Johnny Owen and Benny "Kid" Paret and Frankie Campbell are among the most publicized. They were either fighting for championships or fighting championship caliber guys. We don't hear much about the pugs killed in filthy halls in front of howling, intoxicated punks who don't remotely have the guts to step into a ring. I know what the sports studies say. There are more deaths per capita in football and auto racing and lots of other sports than in boxing. I don't know about that. I just understand that in boxing the primary objective is to destroy the other guy's brain. So don't shovel any crap about people paying big money to watch guys fight defensively.

I like the way my brother Jimmy, the one who knocked me out in a family sparring session and later cared for me, summed up boxing. In a 1995 television interview, as I stood nearby in an eternal and deepening cave, he said: "We won't let dogs fight, we won't let chickens fight, because we care about the animals. But we'll let two men get in the ring and beat each others' brains out."

Sources

Among scores of boxing matches I've attended and countless viewed on television and pay per view, my most riveting memories are the ticketed telecasts of the first Sonny Liston-Floyd Patterson fight, Muhammad Ali-Joe Frazier I and III, Ali-George Foreman, Ray Leonard-Roberto Duran I and II, and Leonard-Thomas Hearns I and II. I also rouse at having been present for the second Ali-Ken Norton match and world title fights between Pipino Cuevas and Pete Ranzany, and Edwin Rosario versus Loreto Garza. Meeting and interviewing Archie Moore and Emanuel Steward, separately, in 1980, remain special experiences.

I would also like to commend the authors and producers of the following important works.

John L. Sullivan – *Strong Boy* by Christopher Klein;

Peter Jackson – *Peter Jackson: A Biography of the Australian Heavyweight Champion* by Bob Peterson.

Jack Johnson – *Unforgivable Blackness: The Rise and Fall of Jack Johnson* by Geoffrey C. Ward; *Unforgivable Blackness: The Rise and Fall of Jack Johnson*, PBS documentary directed by Ken Burns; "Jack Johnson's Jazz Band: Tiger Rag," 1929, YouTube.

Battling Siki – *Battling Siki* by Peter Benson; "Battling Siki," an essay by John Lardner.

Harry Greb – *The Fearless Harry Greb: Biography of a Tragic Hero of Boxing* by Bill Paxton.

Sam Langford – *Sam Langford, Boxing's Greatest Uncrowned Champion* by Clay Moyle.

Tiger Flowers – *The Pussycat of Prizefighting* by Andrew M. Kaye.

Gene Tunney – *Tunney* by Jack Cavanaugh

Oscar Bonavena – KTVN News, Joe Conforte Talks about Bonavena, March 2009; *Las Vegas Review-Journal*, June 29, 2000.

Alexis Arguello – *Sports Illustrated*, October 1985, "Adrift in a Sea of Choices" by Gary Smith; *New York Daily News*, July 1, 2009, article by Bill Gallo; *Village Voice*, July 2, 2009.

Teofilio Stevenson – "The Happiest Man in the World" by Brin-Jonathan Butler.

BoxRec.com and Wikipedia are helpful fact-checking resources.

About the Author

George Thomas Clark is the author of *Hitler Here,* an internationally-acclaimed biographical novel, *The Bold Investor, King Donald, In Other Hands, Paint it Blue, Death in the Ring, Obama on Edge,* and *Echoes from Saddam Hussein.*

Clark also follows the news and sports, exercises daily (albeit delicately), collects contemporary art, enjoys independent movies, and travels to places (most recently Madrid, Mexico City, Quito, Guanajuato, and Aguascalientes) where he can socialize in Spanish.

The author's website is GeorgeThomasClark.com

www.ingramcontent.com/pod-product-compliance
Lightning Source LLC
Chambersburg PA
CBHW021206130626
46554CB00005B/2005